TRAPPED

#3, THE 1000 REVOLUTION

PIPPA DACOSTA

Trapped.

#3, The 1000 Revolution

Pippa DaCosta

Urban Fantasy & Science Fiction Author

Subscribe to her mailing list here.

Novel length.

PRINT ISBN 10: 1518850901

PRINT ISBN 13: 978-1518850905

Version 4.0 (June 2017)

www.pippadacosta.com

SUMMARY_

"When are you going to stop running, Caleb?"

Taking the synth to the casino capital of the nine systems seemed like a great idea at the time, but as Caleb Shepperd's many enemies close in, he only has one way out. He must betray #1001.

Caleb can't make the same mistake twice. Can he?

#1001 has a price on her head. The Fenrir Nine and Chitec will stop at nothing to secure her secrets. The very same secrets that riddle her synthetic mind with faults.

Her systems are failing.

And the one man she's come to trust may prove to be her enemy.

The sizzling, fast-paced, and action packed science-fiction continues in Trapped.

Reading order:

WARNING: R: RESTRICTED
Contains SPACE BATTLES, KILLER AI, AND
INTERGALACTIC ASS-KICKING.
READ AT OWN RISK.

PROLOGUE_

Coded message dispatched to Captain Shepperd of the *Starscream Independent* Tug 606:

'Give Us Hail Lee'

CHAPTER ONE: CALEB_

#1001 COUNTED casino cards like I flew *Starscream*. She made it look difficult—bit her lip, furrowed her brow, hovered her fingertips over the cards as though she wasn't quite sure which one to pick—but she could win the game with her fucking eyes closed. I'd played her a few times on *Starscream* during the jumps to Lyra. She'd progressed from novice to expert in three rounds, then wiped the floor with me. Repeatedly. And she did it in that cool, calculating way of hers, without so much as cracking a smile. Although, somewhere in that head of hers, I was sure she was laughing.

So, her winning at cards was just another day in the black. Only it wasn't. We were in the entertainment capital of the nine systems and had been for several days. Today, we'd already won ten thousand credits. It was time to quit while we were ahead. Right after the synth finished playing her hand game. And maybe a glass of whiskey.

I was standing at the end of the table, arms crossed, watching her like all the others in the small crowd. At some point, the chatter, whispers, and whoops had faded into the background. I was meant to be priming *Starscream* to get us ready to boost off Lyra, but leaving was the last thing on my mind.

She didn't look like a synth. That part of our plan was vital. She'd applied lipstick and that shit women use to darken their lashes; she looked perfect, of course, because her programming couldn't fuck anything up. Her silvery hair hung straight and skimmed the tops of her shoulders. The dazzle of Lyra's lights sparkled in her eyes. Doctor Lloyd, her Chitec technician, had gotten his quick hands on some biolenses so she could slip through the security scans as someone else, someone human. Her act was flawless. She smiled like she meant it—she'd worked on those smiles, and though I knew they were fake, they fooled me every time—but her eyes couldn't really change, not even with the lenses in. They were always cold. Always simultaneously empty while full of knowledge. Too much knowledge, if her erratic behavior of late was any indicator.

But now? Now she was in her fucking element, and I was about to be the first, and probably the only, rich smuggler in the nine systems.

Remembering the plan, I backed away from the table, tucked my hands in my pants pockets, and made for the payment booths. My dark suit meant I blended in with the rich and famous walking the floor of Lyra's more exclusive casinos. The atmosphere of the place assaulted me in a constant barrage of voices, chimes, announcements, laughter, and chinking glasses; on and on it went, chipping away at my patience. Or maybe my restlessness was coming from the fact that I hadn't had a drink in a while. At least not a decent one. Drinking swill to stave off withdrawal didn't count. My abstinence wasn't by choice; we'd run out of credit getting here. Lyra's casinos were my last chance to keep *Starscream* in the black.

"Sir, could you come with us?"

I jerked to a halt, finding two casino security guards blocking my path. Easily twice my size, they sported the kind of bored faces of people itching for a fight to break the monotony of watching rich fuckers gamble their credits away. The larger guy on the right, with hair so short it was barely there at all, eyed me down the length of his nose. His mate, the little guy, scanned the crowd, looking for accomplices, most likely.

"What's this about?" I asked, putting on the kind of haughty arrogance I hoped told these guys I was just like every other too-rich asshole on Lyra.

"The casino would like to discuss this in private, sir," Large said.

Some people glanced my way. The last thing I needed was attention.

I nodded and followed Little through the crowds, away from the booths where I was supposed to meet #1001 in—I checked my comms—fifteen minutes.

"Do you have somewhere to be?" Large asked, following behind.

I flashed him a smile. "A date. Is this going to take long?"

"I doubt it," he drawled with an Old-Earth accent—American, mostly, with a twist of Jotunheim. Lyra was awash with original system immigrants. Old money. Old ethics. Old ways.

I sauntered in line, weaving between the tables toward the elevated exclusive area at the back of the casino. Little and Large hadn't called me by name, so hopefully this was just a routine stop-and-search, in which case I'd be out of the casino in no time. They wouldn't find anything on me. Getting a weapon inside Lyra was impossible due to the fuck-load of scanners. As for my ID, I'd left my personalized comms on *Starscream.* The one on me was an untraceable, out-the-box unit. This wasn't my first Lyra rodeo. I was clean. They had no reason to take this any further, or so I told myself.

We climbed the couple of steps and paused outside the door to one of the private rooms. Large raised his eyebrows when I checked him out a second time and caught him looking at my ass. These men sure looked like casino guards, but as far as I knew, casino guards didn't strip search guests in the back-room luxury pads.

"I don't usually swing that way, but I'll try anything once." I smiled.

He narrowed his eyes, but if he had any kind of retort, he kept it to himself. Little opened the door and ushered me inside. Sparkling chrome mixed with old-world oak greeted me. If the interior designers had been aiming for a pantomime dame's boudoir, they were spot on. Unfortunately, I'd met the dame before: Bruno—Ganymede's drug lord.

Fuck.

My backward step brought me into contact with Large. He shoved me toward the round table, where Bruno had shoe-horned his mass of an ex-pro wrestler body into a creaking chair. The drug lord wore a dapper waistcoat, all dressed up like he might have been on his way to the opera, but smart clothes couldn't hide the grit of Ganymede in his neck creases. Head tilted slightly and fat lips curled in disgust, he squinted at me.

Large's hands roamed over me from behind, over my shoulders, under my arms, and down my waist.

"Oh, honey ..." I purred. "Keep that up and you'll make me hard."

"Shut the fuck up," he grunted, sweeping his hands down my thighs.

"To the left." I widened my stance. "You missed a bit ... There ain't no telling where a guy could conceal a weapon."

Bruno's narrowing eyes met Large's grumbles. "Search him right. That's what I'm payin' you for."

Grumbling some more, Large skimmed his hands up the insides of my legs.

"Yeah, right there."

He muttered a few colorful words and, done with his pathetic search, backed up to join Little in blocking the door.

Bruno snorted and reached for a handful of enriched peanuts from the bowl in front of him. "You were always good for a few laughs, boy."

Past tense, lovely.

Getting those fucking nuts out of the original system cost about as much as putting food on the table for a cycle. Bruno chomped them down like this was Old Earth and nuts still grew on fucking trees. He did it to incite jealousy. All it did for me was incite the urge to bury my fist in his face. If I did, his two guys would be on me. As far as I could see, they weren't armed—only Lyra police had licenses to carry weapons—but Little and Large wouldn't go down easy. I could throw down here, I might even win, but I'd ruin my rent-a-suit.

"What are you doing in Lyra, Shepperd?" Bruno picked a few nuts from his palm and popped them into his mouth.

"Vacation."

"With your second? What's her name ... Francisca?"

I blinked. "Fran no longer works for me."

"Ah." More chewing, his lips smacking together. "Wondered how long it'd take for her to shake you off."

Clearly not in any rush, he sat back, feeding himself those damned nuts. One of these days, I was going to ram those nuts down his throat, but not today.

"So." I grinned. "Was there a point to this? Because if you just wanted to admire the goods, I could've sent you a picture."

"Where's the synth?"

"Synth?"

He dropped the remaining nuts back into the bowl and brushed his hands together. The chair creaked and groaned as he leaned his bulk forward and rested his elbows on the table. I expected some sort of threat, but he flicked his fingers and Little moved in.

I lifted my hands. "Whoa, guys. C'mon—"

He dodged my half-hearted attempt at a right hook, caught my forearm, and yanked it up behind my back, levering me face down onto the table. I winced, cheek pressed against the oak surface, but stayed loose. There's a time and place to fight, and this wasn't it. I tried to straighten up, but Little pushed down between my shoulder blades and held me still.

"A few cycles ago, you stole thirty thousand credits' worth of street-ready *sweet*," Bruno said. "I thought you were the kind of man who always finished a job, but my contact never saw that cargo."

"Yeah, well, fleet picked me up and tossed me in Asgard before I could deliver anything." I angled my head so I could at least see Bruno from my horizontal position. "You didn't exactly inspire me to complete the deal when you sent a fuckin' bounty hunter after Fran."

"Tit for tat, Shepperd. And all because you tried to save a whore?"

"Jesse." I winced as Little leaned into my legs, pinning me down. Bent over as I was, he might as well fuck me; it'd probably be more comfortable.

"After you left, a *life-ever-after* synthetic launched an attack on Ganymede. She took out a dozen fleet troops and left the Mede with your favorite whore. Killed Jesse's pimp too."

"Maybe Jess and the synth are an item?" At least Bruno didn't know I was the one who'd killed his pimp.

"My guys reported being beaten to a pulp in an alley by the same synth. They reckon she saved your hide. So you're not going to try and tell me you've never heard of or seen the synth in question, are you Shepperd?"

There goes that lie. "I remember her. I ain't seen her since."

Little fisted his hand in my hair, yanked my head back, and smacked my face against the table, splitting my forehead open. Blood trickled down the side of my face and pain radiated through my skull, making me reconsider my choice to play it loose. The urge to lash out twitched through my fingers, but our subtle trip to Lyra couldn't involve beating the shit out of Bruno's guys and dumping a whole load of authority interest on me and Starscream. *Keep it simple, get away clean.*

"Try again, Shepperd," Bruno suggested.

"Okay, look. I don't know anything about her. She stowed away on my ship for a while. I was going to sell her. Then that shit with Jesse happened, and fleet stormed Ganymede, and I needed to make a quick getaway ... so I left the synth behind."

He'd obviously been watching me since my arrival on Lyra. #1001 and me had deliberately separated. We'd played our roles, never meeting up in public. If one of us got caught, the other could get away clean. I hadn't actually factored in the possibility that Bruno might be paying Lyra's casinos a visit.

"There's quite a price on your capture, Shepperd. The Candes want your head on a stake. Something about a missing sister. Your name as a smuggler is worth less than dirt. Must be tough getting runs."

Tough was an understatement. We were dead in the black. "I've had a few rough weeks."

His fat lips worked around a smirk. "You have connections to the synth. Don't try and tell me otherwise or you'll find your face buried in this table. I want her. I don't care what you have to do to get her. Chitec spun some tale about a rogue synthetic. They're offering five million for her safe return. I'm going to collect that money, and I'll pay you your ten percent. How does that sound?"

Five million credits for the synth? *Holy shit.* Chen Hung

must have really needed her back to go public with such an offer. Why was she worth so much to him? Was it just the fact she knew he'd killed his daughter, or something else?

Bruno flicked his fingers at Little, who finally let me up. I wiped the blood off my face as best I could and arched an eyebrow at Little's smirk. He'd enjoyed that a little too much for my liking.

Bruno reached inside his waistcoat and tossed a credit card onto the table. "There's fifty on there. Call it a deposit to ensure the job gets done."

"Fifty what?"

"Thousand."

I swallowed, mouth suddenly dry. "And if I can't find her?"

"If you can't or won't do this, then the Candes will be getting a call. I hear they have creative ways of dealing with their enemies." Bruno's smile crawled halfway up his bloated face. "What *did* you do to their sister?"

"No comment." There wasn't a choice here. I had to do this. Or at least, I had to agree to his terms and then think of a way around it once they let me out of this room. I scooped up the card and tucked it inside my jacket pocket. "Give me a few days. I'm sure I'll have the package for you."

"Three days."

"Three days." My heart thudded deep and heavy in my chest.

"I look forward to it." He wagged his fingers at the door, dismissing me. "And you might like to sample some of the goods at *The Jungle*, a club along the strip. I think you'll find a familiar whore there."

I paused at the door and clamped my teeth together. Bruno had won this; I was almost out the door.

Let it go. Once outside I could get my head around every-thing. *Just open the fucking door ...*

Little smiled. I curled my right hand into a fist, itching to punch that fucking smirk through his teeth.

"I'll see you here in three days, Shepperd. Bring the synth, or the Candes will be the ones to greet you."

I opened the door and walked out onto the casino floor. A wash of noise rolled over me, but it might as well have been silence for all I heard. I'd missed the meet with the synth, which meant she'd be on her way back to the ship without me. I exited the casino and grabbed a shuttle pod, then rode in silence through Lyra's sparkling retail strips toward my hotel. The pod skirted around a nearby demonstration. My gaze skimmed over the waving banners and placards. The Lyra authorities kept the rowdy common folk under control, and when they couldn't, fleet usually muscled their way in. Without *Starscream*, I could easily be one of those anonymous faces raging against a world designed to help the rich get richer. Fuck, without *Starscream*, I'd be nothing.

Bruno wanted the synth, and so did the Nine. One offered enough money to set me up for years. Fuck, with credit like that, I could fix *Starscream* up good and proper. Then there was the Nine. They'd pay, but not a lot. Their payment came in the shape of a way to cleanse the shroud of guilt from my soul. If I sold #1001 to Bruno—to Chitec—that guilt would sit on my soul forever. I'd already lived with my guilt long enough to know it wasn't getting any lighter. If I betrayed #1001, the guilt would kill me, same as my brother had warned. Drink, the drugs, the life—it was a death sentence, and I welcomed it, because it was all I deserved. On the plus side, I'd die a rich bastard. Someone somewhere once said: *You can't take it with you*. Apparently, the smartass thought those words might encourage generosity. I figured it meant: *Spend it before the universe takes it away.*

All I had to do was give her up to The Fenrir Nine or Bruno.

I had a third option: not give her up at all. If only that were a real choice. I didn't have enough credit to pay for food, and #1001 would always be hunted, dragging me and *Starscream* down with her.

The pod dropped me off outside my hotel. Given Bruno's parting words, I wasn't entirely surprised to see Jesse outside my door.

"Cale." She smiled a closed, guarded smile as I approached. She was dressed in a sculpted silver silk dress that hugged her curves like a second skin. Her scars were gone and her artificial enhancements had all been tweaked and perfected; she was earning good money again. I'd killed a man to help her escape that life, and here she was, back in the game.

"Let me explain." Either she'd seen the disappointment in my eyes, or she was carrying her own guilt.

I invited her inside, shrugged off my jacket, and tapped the personal interface screen, waking it so I could scan Bruno's card. "Sit down."

She loitered by the door, wringing her hands. Usually she'd be better at hiding any apprehension from her clients. The hand wringing wasn't like her, or maybe I wasn't like other clients.

"Relax," I said. "Who the fuck am I to judge?"

Her shoulders slouched. She let go of her tension with a sigh and made her way to where the cupboards concealed a selection of drinks, clearly knowing her way around this hotel's rooms.

On screen, the contents of the card blipped into existence: 50,000. *Shit.* I tapped "transfer" and watched the numbers switch to my credit account, as easy as that. A twitch of a smile hooked into my lips. *Fifty thousand fucking credits.*

"Jess, share a drink with me."

"You have vodka, some Red, champagne?" She saw my look and smiled. "Whiskey it is."

I switched off the screen, heart fluttering too fast. Fifty thousand was a lot of credits. Ten percent of five million? Five hundred thousand. And all I had to do was hand over the synth.

Jesse handed me the glass. I lifted it in a toast. "To luck."

She frowned and smiled at the same time, giving her expression a comical lilt. She knew I didn't believe in luck, but she still chinked her glass against mine. "Luck."

I leaned against the wall of cupboards, my thoughts wandering to what I could do with my thousands, while Jesse cupped her glass in her hands and gazed out of the window at Lyra's never-ending ocean of lights. There was no sunlight here. Lyra's casino domes occupied a hemisphere bathed in perpetual darkness, though artificial light leeched through the protective glass domes, into the atmosphere. You couldn't see the stars, but you didn't need to. The view from the window sparkled as though those stars had joined us. It should have been beautiful, and it was, but it wasn't for me. I preferred reality, in all of its dirty, downtrodden, war-torn ruggedness.

My wrist comms gently vibrated. I glanced at the screen and saw a message from #1001: DO YOU REQUIRE ASSISTANCE

No question mark. She was too efficient to waste space with punctuation. I dismissed the message with a flick of my wrist. She'd read me like a book the second she saw me. I needed to muddy the telltale signs that I was lying to her.

"There wasn't any work on Mimir," Jesse said. She lost her gaze in her glass, swirling the whiskey like it had all the answers. "I'm only good at one thing."

"You don't need to explain anything to me. We do what we gotta do. Fuck, I know all about that."

"I know, but ... what you did for me ..."

The man I'd killed had beaten her. She thought I'd done it

to save her, but I'd killed the bastard because some things I won't let slide. "You owe me credits for that."

Her pretty doe eyes widened. "I know. I hadn't forgotten. It's part of the reason I came to Lyra. There's always work here for girls who'll fuck for money."

"Is that why you're here?" I spoke into my drink, careful to avoid her gaze.

"After Ganymede, and when fleet attacked Mimir, I wasn't sure if you were alive or dead." She set her glass on a shelf and sashayed forward. Stepping into my personal space, she placed her hand on my chest. Her warm touch seeped through my shirt. Up close, I could admire her elegant eyes and smooth lips. Her beauty was enhanced, but not in the same way as the synth's smooth perfection. A few lines gathered when Jesse smiled and crowded around her eyes. In her sunset years, she'd probably look to be in her late twenties, as long as she kept paying for the enhancements. When you've spent enough time staring at synthetic perfection, it was hard not to notice the imperfections in humanity.

Jesse knew I was an easy mark. We'd danced to the same tune more times than I could count. It was a mutually beneficial arrangement. She got paid, and I got laid. Usually, I'd have been all over her the second she'd arrived. Maybe it was her demure appearance or the fact I was reeling from Bruno's job and subsequent deposit, but I didn't feel particularly inclined to fuck. I already had too much going on in my head, and something in the way she looked at me had me wondering if this was more than a business transaction. A silent plea saddened her gaze, begging me not to turn her away. At least she didn't look at me like the synth, like she already knew my every secret, every grubby little piece of me, and found me decidedly lacking.

Jesse teased open some of my shirt buttons, diverting my thoughts away from #1001.

"Do you want to?" she asked.

No, I thought, surprising even me. I downed my drink and let the burn work its magic all the way through. Maybe a roll in the sack with Jesse would serve up enough emotional bullshit to let me lie to the synth about where I'd been and what I'd been doing. She'd read the lies in my body language. I needed to manufacture an excuse.

"I can loosen you up ..." Jesse peeled back my shirt and trailed the tip of her tongue around a nipple. I closed my eyes and dropped my head back, trying to focus on the soft touch of her tongue. She eased against me, sliding her smooth silk dress along my skin, and whispered, "I don't think I've ever seen you quite so dashing. You look good, yah know. Lyra agrees with you."

Then her light kisses roamed my neck. She slipped her hand inside my shirt and eased it back over my shoulder, revealing more skin for her to explore with her tongue. I should probably have started giving her something back, but my fucking thoughts weren't even in the room.

"What's wrong?" she asked.

"Nothing." I caught her hands in mine. "I'm just distracted."

My wrist comms vibrated again. It'd be the synth, or my brother, wondering where the fuck I was so they could get off Lyra and get to spending the credits the synth had won.

Ignoring her imploring expression, I let go of Jesse, slipped off the comms unit, tossed it onto the shelf, and curled a hand around her waist. The silk transferred her warmth and the feel of her curves and finally things started picking up. I tested her mouth with mine, brushing my lips against hers to see if she'd open up to me. She did. The kiss began oddly tentative and too intimate, and the slight shiver that travelled through her didn't help. Fuck, this meant more to her than a paycheck.

"Jesse—"

She cut me off by mashing her mouth against mine and plunging her tongue in. I threaded my fingers into her hair, meaning to hold her back, but I pulled her close instead, fuelling her kiss with my own and riding the wave of not giving a fuck about anything besides the feel and taste of her. She yanked my shirt out of my pants and dove her hands around my waist and down my lower back to cup my ass and pull me in so fucking tight that pleasure spilled down my cock. Any protest I might have had died right then.

She backed me to the bed, pushed me down, hiked up her dress, and straddled my hips. Her kisses softened and slowed, while her body rocked against mine. I gathered her hair in a hand and gently pulled her to the side so I could nip just below her ear, teasing her. I would've carried on if I hadn't realized that in my fucked-up head, I wasn't kissing Jesse, but the synth. The realization was enough to give me pause. My heart thudded, body awash with pleasure, and I swallowed, debating whether I could do this at all.

Jesse plunged her hand between us and rubbed the heel of her palm against where my cock was straining inside my pants. "Well, this part of you wants me at least."

I gritted my teeth. I was happy enough to let her carry on rubbing right there, but in my head, it wasn't her hand working me.

Holy shit, I'm in trouble.

Sure, it had been a few weeks since I'd had any sex, besides my own hand that was. Fuck, even then I'd been thinking about the synth.

Jesse leaned in and whispered against my lips, "You're thinking about someone else."

"Nah, I—"

"Cale, I'm not new to this. It's okay. Think about her all you like." She averted her eyes, immediately turning her words into lies.

I could have spouted off a load of denials, but she shoved me back, unzipped my pants, and lowered her wet, warm self onto me, taking my cock all the way in. She started rocking, and any denial I'd prepped quickly vanished. I gripped her thighs and urged her on instead of pushing her off. Well, fuck, if she was giving me permission, I wouldn't argue.

I closed my eyes and had no trouble imagining the synth riding me. She'd look at me in that studious way of hers and fuck me senseless, and oh man, I'd let her, because she knew all of me. She knew what made me tick, knew my weaknesses, and she knew exactly how I liked it, because her machine senses would tell her everything. I couldn't hide a damn thing from her and didn't want to. She'd strip me down, reveal the truth, and fuck if that wouldn't be liberating. Just to be me, not the ex-fleet captain, not the fixer who'd do anything for credit, and not even the captain of a beat-up tugship, or the brother who'd gotten left behind. No expectations. No lies. Just me. Now.

The hotel door burst open and a man strode in. Unmistakable cool eyes scanned the room. He wore Chitec grey, tight as a fleet uniform. I'd seen him before—several of him, in fact—the night I'd watched Chen Hung kill his daughter. All 499 like him, lined up like toy soldiers. *A male synthetic.*

I rolled Jesse over, shielding her from the synthetic, and met her wild eyes. "Run!"

The synth's reflection flickered in her wide eyes. He locked his cool hand around my neck, lifting me off Jesse like I weighed no more than a doll. He tossed me aside just as easily. In a blink, I found myself facedown on the floor, wondering how the fuck I'd gotten there. Trying to move hurt. Trying to breathe hurt more. I lifted my head. Warm wetness trailed down the back of my neck. I reached back to cup the throbbing ache in my head. My hand came away wet with blood.

"Where is One Thousand And One?" the male synth

asked, so fucking calm and polite. *Have a nice day, sir. Right after I kick your ass seven ways to Sunday.*

I tried to focus through the pain. He was holding Jesse off her feet, his fingers knotted in her hair. She clutched at his wrist and arm but hardly fought. Fear and agony twisted her face.

"Let her go." I got my hands under me and pushed upright onto my knees, but the room slid sideways.

"Where is she, Captain Shepperd?"

"I—I don't know."

He twitched, at least that's what it looked like, and then he threw Jesse to the floor, where she lay, head and limbs tilted at odd angles. Her fingers contracted and her foot jerked, and then she went still. Panic, fear, confusion, they all screeched to a halt inside my head. I shoved off the floor and managed to climb onto unsteady legs.

"You just made an enemy of a fixer, you synthetic fuck."

His straight face betrayed nothing. "Take me to One Thousand And One."

"Fuck you." I didn't have any weapons, didn't even have my comms. He'd snapped Jesse's neck in less than a second. I couldn't fight him. I knew that, and so did he.

I tried to tuck my junk away while swaying on the spot and managed it—barely. If I were about to die here, I'd die with some dignity. "C'mon, you fake freak. I'm ready to die. Are you?"

He stepped toward me and I bolted for the door. I managed to get halfway down the hallway before he slammed me against the wall from behind. I went down hard, sprawling face first, and then stilled as he leaned a knee into my back. The punch to the kidneys almost tore my consciousness away. A shock of cold sweat followed hot nausea. If I threw up and blacked out, there was every chance I'd die right here.

"Where is she?"

"Yah know ..." I coughed and spat blood on the polished marble floor. "I've always wondered: Can synthetics even get it up—"

"Is One Thousand And One worth more to you than your life?"

"That's a very astute question."

"Halt! Police! Refrain and desist immediately!"

Thank fuck for that. I blinked through the haze of pain and sickness to find the hallway choked with Lyra cops, all armed with pulsers. I'd been on the pronged end of those weapons on a few occasions, and every time I'd vowed never again. The electrical pulses would make a synthetic think twice.

The pressure of the synth's knee lifted off my back, allowing me to breathe around bruised ribs.

"Face the wall, sir."

The cops ventured closer. I stayed down as I watched the synth calmly oblige. His cooperation didn't last. He broke into a run and burst through the line of cops at the far end of the hallway. They fired their pulsers, but the synth was fast— faster than they'd expected. Some chased after him. After that, I didn't much care. He was away from me, and by some fucking miracle, I was still breathing.

"We've got a body," came a shout from my hotel room.

I closed my eyes, willing unconsciousness to scoop me up and carry me away. It didn't, which was fucking typical. So I suffered through physical agony as I waited for the EMTs to arrive. As for the emotional shit, I didn't let it touch me. Not yet. First, I had to get the fuck off Lyra so I could take a timeout and think my way out of this mess.

Jesse ... Goddammit. I'd kill that synthetic bastard and make him realize there wouldn't be a *life-ever-after* for him.

"IT'S BEEN TOO LONG," Commander Brendan Shepperd said, pacing the few short strides from one side of the cargo hold to the other. The sound of his boots on the grating echoed through the empty space.

I'd returned to the late hours of yesterday evening with the credits I'd won, expecting to find Captain Shepperd inside. He'd been at the last table, watching me like the rest of the crowd, but he hadn't made our scheduled meeting and had yet to return to *Starscream*. With every Lyra hour and every one of his strides, the commander's anxiety levels spiked, and as if by proxy, so did mine.

"He said to leave if one of us didn't make it back."

The commander stopped dead. "Are you prepared to leave my brother here?"

"It was an order," I replied.

He made a noise like a frustrated growl. "You know, better than most, that some orders are meant to be disobeyed."

Brendan loved his brother. He may not have acted like it whenever they were in the same room together, but it was there, in his tight pacing and quick glances at the exit door.

They rarely spoke except to bicker, but apparently, that was normal behavior for the Shepperd brothers.

"I got something," James announced as he entered the hold via the internal door. He handed me a newspad.

One man was arrested and another is still at large after a body was discovered at the Sharline Hotel yesterday evening. The deceased is believed to be a female escort with links to local property and business owner, Bruno Divalsh. The names of the victim and assumed perpetrator are not being released at this time. Reports cannot confirm or deny whether the man in custody has been charged with murder. Lyra Police have asked for anyone who may have overheard an altercation at the hotel to come forward.

"Bruno," I said. The name echoed around us.

"After what you told me about the events on Ganymede," James began, sweeping his jacket back to rest his hand on his hip, "Captain Shepperd may be the man in custody or the man at large."

The commander took the pad from me and skimmed it. "Dammit."

"It would explain why he's not here," James said. "And why he hasn't contacted us."

The commander lifted his gaze, his darting eyes searching the hold for answers. "If he's in custody, the police will be watching this ship. I can't let them see my face. James?"

The doctor flinched. "What?"

"Go to the Police Department and see if Caleb is there."

"Me? I ... I wouldn't know—"

"I'll go," I said. James was already a bundle of frayed nerves at the suggestion of striding into the police station and lying. My lies were faultless. "I will ascertain who's there and if the captain is on the run."

We'd tried his comms with no reply. He'd either abandoned it somewhere so it couldn't be tracked, or the police had confiscated it.

"Soften your appearance," Bren ordered in his typical commander tone that crept in when he wanted to distance himself from events. "Like you did for the casinos. The people of Lyra may not immediately recognize a synthetic among them, but the police are a little more perceptive."

Fifteen minutes later, I was back in my high-end pencil skirt suit, with my hair clipped back—the picture of sophisticated elegance on three-inch heels. James avoided meeting my eyes while I confirmed to the commander and him that I'd report back as soon as I knew where we stood.

I left *Starscream* and caught a shuttle pod to downtown Lyra. Like the rest of the entertainment planet, downtown throbbed with people high on the buzz that infused Lyra's strips. Even the police department building glowed blue at its edges. Everything on Lyra shone. When we'd first arrived, I'd let the light bathe my senses. But after a few days, the light now burned and grated against my internal processes.

The on-duty officer at the desk barely gave me a second glance. "Sign in."

I scribbled a nonsense signature that simply said "One"— James's preferred name for me. "I'm hoping you might be able to help me."

He lifted his gaze at the sound of my cultured voice and finally noticed me. Something like recognition widened his tired eyes, but his heartbeat remained steady.

"Yes?" he drawled, his Lyra accent sharp and tinny.

"Do you have a man here by the name of Caleb Shepperd?"

He checked behind me at the two people waiting in the plastic chairs. One was a young woman who was picking at her nails, while the other appeared to be asleep. I'm not sure what the officer expected to find, an accomplice perhaps, but when he returned his gaze to me, his suspicion had faded.

"I'll check for you, ma'am."

He turned his chair away and tapped a few commands into his holoscreen. His heartbeat remained steady, so I could assume all of this was routine, but the police were trained in dealing with extenuating circumstances. I couldn't expect his physiological reaction to be the same as a civilian's. There was every chance he'd recognized me as a synthetic. Fleet usually had a substantial presence in Lyra airspace, although the captain had commented on how their numbers appeared to have thinned. Either way, *Starscream* had already stayed docked too long.

"Yes, he's being processed. If you'd like to wait a while, you'll be able to see him."

"How long?"

He checked his screen. "An hour. Maybe two."

"It's just ... I'm his wife, and well ... I really need to see him."

His eyebrow arched. Despite delivering my lie with perfect cadence, he didn't believe me. Something in my act wasn't right, be it the clothes, or the accent, or me.

"His wife?"

"Yes." I chewed on my lip and played with the sleeve of my jacket. "We were recently married, as of yesterday ..." I added a giggle. "Kinda trick ... right?"

He lifted his chin as my lie slipped into place. It had been the accent—too clean for Lyra. I made a mental note to soften my dialect as well as my appearance. "He'll be out soon enough, ma'am."

I took a seat and waited, pretending to watch the video stream in the far left-hand corner while surreptitiously watching both the entrance doors and back corridors. I didn't believe he'd notified fleet, but that didn't ease my itching restlessness.

I reached behind my neck and touched the slightly raised Chitec brand. It didn't used to bother me, but I was changing—the way I processed and compartmentalized information, the way I dreamed, and the way I woke and choked on words my internal protocols prohibited me from saying. I wasn't just a synthetic. I was one more.

A slither of unease moved beneath my polymer skin. The sensation wasn't synthetic. Nothing in my processes accounted for it. I'd felt it before, when being watched. A quick scan of my surroundings yielded nothing unusual.

Slamming doors lifted me from my roaming thoughts, and I found Caleb Shepperd sauntering down the hall. He sported a medi-strip and bruise above his left eye, and a few scratches about his face. I scanned his vitals. His heart rate had tripled in the space of a few strides, almost as though he were afraid—of me. I hadn't seen that response in him for a few weeks and believed we'd moved beyond fear. My scans also indicated he was in pain—his lower back, judging by his gait. A few splotches of dark blood marred his white shirt. Caleb Shepperd was a mess, physically and mentally. At my conclusion, a curious twitch of sensory pain darted through me. The pain wasn't tangible. It didn't have a direct source and wasn't something I could dismiss with a simple instruction. It was new and worthy of later study. Human empathy. I shut the sensation away, closed my mental processes around it, and kept it safe before it could escape me, as though I were cupping a butterfly in my hands.

With a breezy, enthusiastic smile, I stood and said, "Honey …"

Captain Shepperd had called women the same often enough, usually in jest.

He blinked and frowned in quick succession—surprise,

confusion—then he caught the officer watching us and adopted a smile that mirrored mine. "You came?"

It sounded like a question, and I wasn't sure if he'd meant it as one. "Sure. I wasn't gonna leave you here." My accent gave him pause, but his sideways smile told me he appreciated it.

"Sign here." The officer dumped an electronic form in front of the captain, who dutifully planted his thumbprint on the document. "This here's to say you have no intention of leaving Lyra. Should you get any ideas about leaving the enter-tainment capital of the nine systems, you'll lose your bail money, and me and the boys get to spend a wild weekend of drinking and gambling on you."

Shepperd grunted a derogatory term, turned on his heels, and strode through the department doors.

We'd barely descended two steps when he growled, "What the fuck, synth?"

Anger pulled his voice tight, but there was a lot more hidden in its resonance: fear, as well as despair. He tried to hide it, control it, but in doing so, his efforts only further alerted me to their presence, and once I knew they were there, I went hunting for more physical hints.

"You shouldn't be here," he continued. "I told you, if anything went wrong, you were to get the fuck off Lyra. Take the credits and go."

We reached the strip and he hailed a pod. The automated glass bubble veered off its track and rocked to a halt in front of us. Its curved door slid upward.

Cocooned in silence, I sat opposite Shepperd. He slumped in his seat, knee jumping while he stared through the glass dome. His dark eyes reflected Lyra's lights. He barely blinked and barely moved but for his jittery knee.

I'd gathered enough data to know the basics about the events that had transpired during the past few hours, but I needed to hear his recall to complete the picture. Much about his data didn't align. I'd spent enough time around the captain to know that if I were a person, my instincts would be telling me that something was off with Caleb Shepperd's behavior. "What happened?"

"Jesse ..." His voice caught. "She turned up at my hotel room. Probably sent by Bruno to keep an eye on me." He struggled to get the words out, guarding them behind walls and only letting a few through. He still didn't look at me. "She's ... she was working for him. Again." His vitals skipped and jumped. "We er ..."

There was that hitch again.

"Caleb."

He darted his gaze to me like I'd slapped him. He didn't like hearing his name from my lips, but it worked to focus him.

"Are we in any immediate danger?" I asked.

"Fuck yeah. The cops don't believe me, even though they saw him. They think we were working together, that a threesome got out of hand. They charged me with her fucking murder." He laughed—an ugly, broken sound. "I didn't kill her, synth."

The truth in his words shone like a beacon of confidence through the storm of mixed messages his body was broadcasting. "What man?"

His gaze locked on mine, half-accusatory. The rest of the accusation arrived in his voice. "One of *your* kind."

My kind?

"A synthetic killed her?" If I'd had a heart, it would have been hammering hard. As it were, countless processes and scenarios spilled into my thoughts. "That's not possible."

"Fuck you, synth. That's what the cops keep telling me. Of course it's fucking possible. Fucking protocols and bullshit failsafes. They're all killers, every last one thousand and one of them. Even you. Especially you."

His words struck at a part of me that didn't exist in programming, that intangible part where emotions were born, and it hurt. The pain was different this time but as worthy of study as empathy. I swallowed and closed my eyes, regaining control inside of a second. "Did he have a number or call himself by a name?"

"We didn't have time for proper introductions while he was beating the shit out of me." Hatred burned through the anger in his eyes. Hatred for me? I tilted my head. No, hatred for my kind, for the others who looked exactly like me, and for what I represented.

"We should return to *Starscream*," I said, careful to keep my voice leveled and controlled. He couldn't know how his words hurt, not yet. None of them could know until I'd studied the data and concluded what it meant to be ... me.

"No."

"No?"

He rubbed a hand down his face. "I just ... I need to get my shit together. I can't go back there and face my brother's questions. I need time—just some time, synth." He bowed forward, resting his elbows on his knees, and threaded his fingers into his hair. "*Starscream* will never get clearance codes for departure, not with me on bail. The docking umbilical won't release without those codes. She's as grounded as I am until I can deal with this."

"Brendan is worried."

Caleb bowed his head once more and mumbled, "He should be."

I had more questions. I wanted to know everything about the synthetic who'd attacked Jesse—what he'd said and what he wanted—but Shepperd was in no condition to withstand a barrage of questions.

We rode in silence. Outside the pod, Lyra's permanent darkness lightened and the lights faded away as we approached the rim of the entertainment domes. We eventually alighted the pod in a rundown strip where the residential blocks were in the process of being torn down and others rebuilt. Empty high-rises stood like tombstones, reaching toward the concave domes high above. Black windows watched me like a thousand eyes. The unease I'd experienced in the police department hadn't waned. It crawled across my skin like thousands of tiny pinpricks.

"What is this place?" I could have searched the datacloud but didn't want to touch it here, as though the cloud itself might flood the insidious sensation through me.

"Nowhere. Sidelined developments from a property boom that never lived up to the dream," Caleb replied, opening the door to a rundown hotel lobby. So rundown, in fact, that nobody manned the front desk. He leaned over, snatched himself a keycard, left his thumbprint on a dust-covered guestbook, and sauntered toward the elevator.

I eyed the abandoned foyer and the descending elevator numbers with concern. "Considering the state of disrepair, I'd recommend the stairs."

Caleb huffed a dry laugh and headed for the stairs. "You look shocked, synth." His voice ricocheted up the stairwell. "And there I was thinking you were the type of girl who'd rough it anywhere."

Girl, not machine. He didn't seem to notice his slip, but I held on to it and replayed the sound with every step. These occasional slips mattered. I collected and cherished them, and then, when alone, I examined them all over again. James— Doctor Lloyd—seemed to believe it was good to fixate on human responses, but I wasn't convinced. I didn't know why I did the things I did, and slowly, piece by piece, step by step like the stairs we were climbing, I wondered if I might be breaking apart.

Shepperd entered the room matching his keycard number.

The lights automatically brightened, revealing a made-up hotel room complete with stained carpeting and sheets faded to gray. I wrinkled my nose. Fingerprints from several previous occupants dotted the layers of dust. Shepperd rolled up his sleeves, grabbed the chair from beneath a desk, and dumped it by the window. He moved about the room with familiarity. He'd been here before. *A smuggler's safe house?* I closed the door and watched him sink into the chair with a wince.

"You just going to fucking stand there and read me? Tell me I'm a wreck, that I'm hurting?" He looked over his shoulder. "I can see it in your eyes, synth. You have a million things you want to say but won't, not until you think I can handle it." He faced away from me to look out the window at Lyra's sparkling strips. "You don't need to be here. Go back to Bren if you want."

"The synthetic will try again."

"He'll have to find me first, and this place is off the map, so long as we don't use comms. Comms can be backward traced."

He kept his back to me, the chair angled away. I couldn't read him and he knew it. What did he have to hide? I already knew he was barely functioning.

"The synthetic wanted you, One Thousand And One," Shepperd said, his words soft in the quiet.

"You didn't tell him where I was." I crossed the floor to the window and stood beside him but kept my gaze ahead.

"He was going to kill me whether I told him or not." Quieter still … almost a whisper this time. His heart slowed as the weight of events pushed down on him.

Haley. Adelina Candelario. Francisca Olga. And now Jesse. I didn't need a myriad of processes to understand the anguish he was experiencing. "Grief is perfectly normal in such circumstances."

He waited a beat and then chuckled dryly. "You're so fucking cold, you know that? I don't need you to diagnose me.

Stop trying to figure me out. Stop all the fucking poking and prodding through every word I say, every goddamn expression. I don't need a damn psychiatrist."

"What do you need, Caleb?"

"How about a friend?"

I turned my head and looked down at him. Slouched in the chair, with Lyra's lights blanketing him, he didn't seem as vulnerable as he should have. He exuded a resolute stubbornness where others would be floundering, as though the more he got knocked down, the more he'd get back up and be stronger for it. He looked back at me, his eyes guarded and his heartbeat steady.

"Bruno offered me five hundred thousand credits to hand you over."

That might explain the mixed messages. "Did you accept?"

"Yes."

He didn't look away, didn't falter. His gaze almost challenged me to retaliate in some way. He wanted me to argue, to fight, to accuse him. It's what Fran would have done. But I wasn't Fran, and I had no intention of falling into his trap. The offer, the money, him—it all made sense. It was logical. He should have accepted. What didn't make sense was why he was telling me.

His sigh came out shaky and weak. "He gave me a fifty-thousand deposit, which the cops now have to ensure I don't fuck off. I never had so much money in my account." He flicked his fingers. "And now it's gone."

"If you intend to hand me over, why tell me?"

"Because ..." He wet his lips and slumped back in the chair, rubbing his forehead.

I faced away again, allowing him to speak without feeling pressured to say the right thing beneath my glare. His heartbeat increased.

"Fuck, I don't know. It sounded sweet, all that credit. It'd change my life. But folks around me keep dying. The choices I make, they never turn out right. So, you get to decide. You're the machine. Tell me what the best course of action is."

The solution was more complicated than that. I didn't have the answers he was seeking. "I don't have all the data. The smallest error could result in an undesirable outcome."

"That sounds like a cop-out."

"I can present options and solutions to likely scenarios, but you aren't telling me everything, Captain. You're deliberately omitting certain facts, facts that you're struggling with. Until you tell me the truth, there is little point in me advising you."

I didn't need to look at him to know my words had struck him close to his heart, similar in the way to how his words had hurt me.

"I've been charged with murder, I've spent Bruno's deposit, and he's going to hand me over to the Candes if I don't bring you in. I'm trapped, synth. Every way I turn, everywhere I look, there ain't no good way out."

He was right. Knowing what I did, there was no way out for him, and perhaps that was how it should be. He'd been running for a long time. Now his past was catching up with him, and there was justice in that. Order. A sense of fairness. People had died because of his greed. Shouldn't he pay? But in the brief time I'd spent on his tugship, I'd learned the nine systems didn't function that way. Life wasn't neat; it wasn't controlled. Life was random, and unfair, and illogical. I had once wanted him dead, but it had wounded me to think of him so.

Run, One Thousand And One. Run! Chen Hung's parting words haunted me. This wasn't just about Caleb. The synthetic wanted me. Chen Hung wanted me. I hadn't yet been able to free the vital information from my head. Chen Hung, Chitec CEO, was a synthetic, and nobody knew but me. That information was worth more than Caleb or *Starscream* and her crew. I couldn't be caught, not until I'd spoken the truth. There had to be a way to escape.

"I may be able to hack into the port authority controls via the cloud."

Caleb leaned forward, eyes widening. "I'm listening."

"I don't know if it's possible, but, similar to the way I harvest information from the cloud, I could attempt to enter the port authority data. Once inside, there's a chance I could manipulate it, providing I can find *Starscream's* docking commands. It's a slim chance. In all likelihood, there are firewalls that prevent unauthorized access, but we already know I'm not a typical synthetic unit. It's certainly not legal and could result in the arrest of your crew."

"Are there any other risks?"

"No. I don't believe so."

"Do it."

It wouldn't stop the Candes or Bruno from hunting us, but it would get *Starscream* in the air. I closed my eyes and mentally reached for the cloud. Like a dream, the cloud embraced me, wrapping my processes in knowledge-rich data, but within moments, the dream darkened. The lingering sensation of being watched amplified a hundredfold and surged over me, sinking in its claws to drag me under. I tried to disengage from the cloud and pull back, but the oily presence tightened, holding me close, refusing to let me go ...

Human sensations of panic and fear shattered my organized attempt to flee so that I flailed uselessly in the stream of knowledge. Whatever had a hold of me didn't hesitate. It locked onto me with machine precision and dragged me under.

CHAPTER THREE: CALEB_

WHILE THE SYNTH stood cool and immobile, part of her off searching the datacloud, I studied her smartly dressed figure. She rocked her skirt suit like a fucking celebrity and was just as untouchable. After the chaos of Jesse's murder and the subsequent police meat grinder, I'd almost forgotten I was supposed to hand the synth over to Bruno in two days. I might have been able to fool her, had the male synthetic not fucked up my plans, but as I'd suspected, she'd read me like a book the second she'd seen me and had known I was hiding a fuck-load of things from her.

I had to tell her the truth, at least some of it. I wasn't going to tell her how the Nine also wanted her, or how I'd been thinking of her while Jesse was fucking me. That was too much emotional shit I didn't need right now. My half-truths seemed to have placated her; she would get us off Lyra, if she could hack the port authority. For now, that would have to do. If I could get back-in-black, maybe I could think straight again. As is, I could barely string a fucking sentence together without wanting to throw a punch or throw up. The synth would tell me that I was having a psychological breakdown. Fuck her constant reports and her detached bubble of not giving a fuck.

I slid my gaze down her shoulder and over the neat curves of her jacket where it hugged her chest and the sweet hollow of her waist, and down those athletic legs. *Fuck.* I knew she wasn't real. Her and her five hundred sisters looked the same. The real *her*—#1001, Haley, or whoever she really was—existed in her head somewhere, trapped between programming and memories. But I could *look* to distract myself for a few seconds. I shifted in the chair and adjusted my pants as I started getting hard. It occurred to me that this was probably a fucked-up thing to be doing—getting my rocks off while she was plugged into some metaphysical data-plane—but I didn't give a shit.

Then I remembered how the male synth had broken Jesse's neck as easily as snapping a twig and my distraction technique withered. That man—that machine had killed without blinking. He—it had felt nothing in that moment between her life and her death. All one thousand synthetic units were the same: Cold. Hard. Machines. I'd tortured myself with the image of Jesse's death while sitting in the jail cell. The last moments of her life had consisted of fucking an asshole smuggler who hadn't even been thinking about her. I'd been low before, but this time I wasn't sure I could possibly hate myself more.

The synth collapsed.

She just fell, as though someone had unplugged her.

"Hey!" I dropped to my knees and gripped her cool face in my hands.

Her fucking eyes were open but unfocused. When I waved my hand in front of her, she didn't flinch.

"Holy shit." I patted her cheek and then lightly slapped her, but she didn't register a thing. "Synth...?" Was she dead? "Synth? C'mon ... you can't do this right now."

Nothing. I reached for a pulse point on her neck and then wondered what the fuck I was doing. She didn't have a heart to beat.

"Is there an on switch? A reset fucking button?!"

How the fuck do these synthetics work? I spied her wrist comms. If I called Doctor Lloyd, I'd risk pinging our location and the male synthetic could trace us. What if she was dying? No way. I couldn't deal with this. Not now. Not again.

"Fuck ..." I leaned in close and peered into her shallow eyes. "Are you in there?"

She wasn't breathing, but that didn't mean anything. She didn't *need* to breathe.

"Synth ..." I whispered, cupping her face, forcing her to look through me. "Haley?" Nothing.

Shit.

I unlatched her wrist comms, adjusted it to my own wrist, and pinged the doc. "Lloyd. There's a problem with the synth."

"Oh"—he exhaled hard—"she found you."

"She was hacking into the port authority using the datacloud and now she's out cold."

"What? You'll have to be more specific. Why was she—"

"How can I be more specific? She's lying on the floor, and I'm not getting anything from her. No breathing. Nothing. She looks ... dead." Shit, my voice cracked, and he heard it.

His voice softened. "It's okay, Captain. I suspect it's a hard reset. Although I don't know why she'd execute a reset in public. Where are you?"

"I can't tell you that."

"Why not?"

"It's safer for you if you don't know."

"Was she experiencing an episode?" His tone had hardened; clearly, this was my fault and he didn't trust a thing I said. His opinion of me hadn't improved of late.

"No." I'd witnessed her episodes. She'd struggle with whatever was going on inside her head, mumbling random nonsense about protocols, and then she'd fall quiet. This wasn't that. "She went into the cloud to help ..."

"When she comes around, bring her straight back to the ship. I have some new equipment, and this isn't normal behavior."

I ended the call and settled my gaze on the synth's perfect face. With her blank look and flat gaze, this was too much like Jesse. There was nobody home. Grief clawed at my insides, trying to rip me apart. Hot and cold shivers had a hold of me, like some drug comedown, but this was all my own fucked-up nightmare. I deserved this. I scrambled back and made it to the bathroom before heaving up what little there was in my guts.

The synth found me sitting back against the bathroom wall maybe fifteen minutes—maybe fifty minutes—later. She stood in the doorway, judging me with her perfectly impassive face, spearing her gaze right through me. She'd see the wetness on my cheeks, the cruel twist of my lips. I didn't know what she thought, but I did care, and that made her indifference so much worse.

"He's here," was all she said, and then all hell broke loose.

———

I heard the noise first, like an explosion. The male synth slammed into #1001, and in a blink, she was gone from the doorway. A breath later, the sound of shattering glass spurred me into action. I came out of the bathroom, my heart in my throat, and saw #1001 clinging to the wrong side of the window frame. Lyra's dazzling lights backlit her, and her silvery hair flared around her face. The male synth drew his fist back. She'd never hold on. I knew from experience that he hit like a truck. I had a broken rib and bruised kidney to prove it. I was on him before I'd considered running. Hooking my arm around his neck, I yanked him back, but all it did was divert all of his attention onto me, and I found myself smashed into the floor, pain snapping up my back all over again. I coughed and tasted blood. *Shit.*

#1001 jumped him from behind, locking her legs around his waist and her arms around his throat. Her face was startlingly calm as she jerked his head back, clearly trying to snap his neck. He clawed at her shoulders and hair, turning and staggering on the spot. Then he slammed her backward into the wall, bringing half the plasterboard down around them.

Run. I saw the order in her eyes as her gaze snapped to mine. The male synth rammed her back again and again to loosen her grip, and he did it all with the most serene and empty expression.

Run, right, because there was no way in the nine systems I could beat him. Knowing the odds were stacked against me had never stopped me before. If there was one thing I knew how to do right, it was take a beating.

I rolled onto my side and staggered to my feet. Scanning the room for any sign of a weapon only reminded me how hopeless this was. *There has to be something!*

"Caleb, go!"

The male synth stilled and brought his gaze around to me. He'd heard the concern skitter through #1001's tone and had found her weakness: me.

For the second time in less than twenty-four hours, I ran. I darted out the room, down the hall, and caught the open elevator car. I punched at the lobby button in time to see the male synth stride out of my room and bear down on me. My bruised lungs and broken chest burned. The air-con hummed and the lights beat their heat over me, but the doors didn't fucking move. I jabbed the close button repeatedly and considered darting for the stairs when the doors finally rumbled closed with a rickety jolt.

I fell back against the panel, panting hard. Where was #1001? I couldn't outrun this machine. The only weakness I knew he had was the cold. #1001 had nearly met her end when her temperature had dropped on Mimir. Lyra's temperature plummeted outside the domes. I could survive maybe a minute. The cold would surely kill him, but I didn't know if it was possible to get through the domes anywhere besides the atmosphere domelocks.

The sounds of grinding gears were promptly followed by a hefty jolt. The elevator ceiling caved in, raining glass and metal from above. Darts of pain dashed through my shoulders. I covered my face and felt sharp stabs slice across my forearms. His hand shot through my meager defenses, curled around my neck, and lifted me clean off my feet. This was how Jesse had died. He'd break my neck—

He has the same eyes as #1001, electric blue and dead cold.

#1001 dropped through the gap in the ceiling and swung a kick into his back. He released me and turned on her. Wedged into the corner, all I could do was watch as they landed blow after blow. She tore into him the way I'd seen her move in the alley on Ganymede, only this was almost too quick for me to track and a thousand times more brutal. She'd slam his head into the side of the car, only for him to kick her legs out, but even when she fell she lashed out. Pure, unfiltered fury twisted her perfect face, twisting her artificial beauty into something else, something deadly. Something real. And he barely blinked. Through it all, she blocked his route to me, every time, until he swung her around and slammed her into the panel hard enough to buckle it. She fell, motionless.

Fuck. "What's your number?" I asked as he straightened and stepped over #1001. Maybe I could stall him and find something, anything, to stop him.

"My number is irrelevant," he said in precise Janus Station English. "My name is Tarik, and you will ensure One Thousand And One comes with me."

A fragment of rebar burst through his chest, peppering my face with synthetic blood. He looked down, face blank, before dropping to his knees.

The elevator car *dinged* and the doors rumbled open to reveal an empty lobby.

I snatched #1001's cool hand and dragged her out of the mangled wreckage. We stumbled down the steps and ran. #1001 loped beside me, splatters of blood bright on her pale face and hair. She veered right, gaze intent. I followed, trusting her to get us somewhere safe. Around the next partially constructed high-rise, she hailed an empty pod and we ducked inside. I twisted in the seat, glaring out the back, waiting for that son of a bitch to come running after us.

"He can't follow," she said, voice obscenely calm. "I punctured his power core. He is running on reserve power and will need to return to the nearest Chitec service station for repairs."

I continued watching the strip and only turned once the crowds started to build as we encroached on Lyra's more populated districts.

"Are you hurt anywhere besides the obvious physical wounds?" she asked.

"No more than usual."

She, on the other hand, looked like she'd been dragged behind a shuttle. Her jacket was torn, her legs were scraped, and her knuckles were bleeding. "You?"

"Considerably," she deadpanned.

"Can you make it back to *Starscream*?"

"Yes, though it won't do us any good. I couldn't hack the port authority. Tarik ambushed me in the datacloud."

I didn't care to ask how the fucking synthetic could be

waiting in the cloud. The *how's* didn't matter. We were trapped, and he'd come for her, and me, again.

"Okay ... that's ..." I scratched around my head for something coherent and failed, my sentence fading away. Everything was fucked up, that's what it was, but I had to think, to move forward, even if all I wanted to do was stop. "*Starscream's* hull is impenetrable to any weapon Lyra's finest can muster and no projectile weapons are permitted here. He'd need cutting equipment to get in, and they don't sell that shit in casinos. We're safer on the ship than anywhere else."

Her eyelashes fluttered and her focus drifted.

"Synth?" I swapped sides to sit beside her. "Don't switch off again. I'm not dragging your unconscious ass back to *Starscream*."

Her lips twitched. "Did my nonresponsive state frighten you, Captain?"

She already knew the answer. "Fuck no. I was contemplating leaving you there when you found me heaving my guts up in the bathroom."

We fell into an uneasy quiet, interrupted only by the electric hum of the pod and the occasional jolt as it jumped its tracks.

"I gotta say," I mumbled, "this is one of my more eventful trips to Lyra."

"Do you come here often?"

Some chat-up lines never die. I had to smirk, though she'd never get the reference if I tried explaining it to her. "Sure. Lyra runs are lucrative. The heavy fleet presence scares off novice smugglers."

"Tarik will not stop," she said with a soft sigh. "It is clear he's been tailing me since Janus, probably utilizing my every connection with the datacloud."

"Following the breadcrumbs."

She gave me that blank look, the one she often used when

I'd reference something she didn't understand. I smiled, knowing an explanation would be more trouble than it was worth. "Everyone wants a piece of you, synth."

"Do you?"

My smile slipped. I wasn't entirely sure what she meant. "Why are the nine systems' most notorious fighting over you? It's gotta be more than Chitec's reward credits." Better to ask that question than to answer the one in her eyes.

"Because I have k-knowledge." The stammer wasn't the first I'd heard from her. It happened whenever the subject of whatever secret shit she had in that head of hers mentioned. If I pushed for more, she'd breakdown, lose herself to the memory of what had happened to her on Janus. Her past couldn't help us.

I settled back in the seat and let my eyes close. The image of Jesse dangling in Tarik's grip immediately spilled into my thoughts. I jolted at the moment he killed her and snapped my eyes open, my blood rushing in my ears. #1001's cool fingers brushed across the back of my hand and curled into my palm. I didn't look, didn't move. She gave my hand the slightest squeeze. The gesture was entirely human, a selfless gesture offering comfort. It terrified me.

CHAPTER FOUR: #1001_

THE SPIDER-CRAWL of Tarik's attention skittered over me as soon as we stepped from the pod. He somehow simultaneously existed in the cloud and here, and watched me through both locations. Dismissing my own diagnostic warnings regarding my general state of disrepair, I scanned the busy dockside but couldn't see him and had no intention of delving back into the cloud to find him. He was there, but holding back. A warning. He knew where we were.

Starscream's overhanging front section loomed high above us. Her hold was closed, but the personnel pressure door would be unlocked. "Get inside."

Shepperd ignored my words but picked up on my tone and glared into the crowds. "Where is he?"

"Close." I mentally cut my link to the cloud, severing the permanent connection with nine systems' worth of knowledge, and turned my back on Lyra. My internal processes were curiously quiet now that I was isolated in my own head.

Following Caleb up the personnel ramp, I noticed his hesitation outside the pressure door. He clamped a hand over the latch and sucked in a deep breath. He straightened his back and lifted his chin, the muddle of emotion he'd worn on his face since the police department vanishing. Then he pushed inside his ship's hold.

"Oh my, what happened to you two?" James came forward but pulled up short as Shepperd brushed by him.

"Give me a while to get my shit together and I'll debrief you."

His brother came through the opposite door and for the smallest of moments, relief brightened Bren's face. Then in the next step thunder replaced the light in his eyes. "Caleb-Joe, what did you do?"

I pulled *Starscream's* outer pressure door closed, then locked and sealed it tight. Nothing would be getting inside without industrial cutting gear.

Caleb's sharp laugh sliced through the empty cargo hold. "Fuck, I haven't even been tried yet, but you already know I'm guilty."

I eased forward, my processes feeding me the information that the brothers' emotional states were quickly disintegrating. James darted his gaze all over me with questions in his eyes. I ignored him.

"Who was she?" Bren asked, adamant disappointment as plain as day on his face.

A muscle fluttered in Caleb's cheek, and when he spoke, his voice came out flat and controlled. "Jesse …"

Bren's brown eyes widened. He'd known Jesse. They'd met when I'd helped them escape Ganymede. They'd spent time together after fleet had destroyed the Mimir warehouses. His heartbeat jumped. "When will you realize you can't go on like this?"

Caleb lifted his chin. "It wasn't my fault. Bruno—"

Bren exploded. His vitals flared hot and fast, and he moved in on Caleb. He loomed over his younger brother in a way I'd never seen from the commander. "Fran?! The Cande girl!" His right hand flexed into a fist. "Christ, Caleb. Take some responsibility. You killed them!"

Caleb stepped back, just the one step, but the submission didn't last. He swung a fast and tight right hook, punching Bren square in the jaw. The commander reeled and lunged.

I was between them before either could stop me. I shoved Caleb back and held him there, hand splayed on his chest while he glared through me at his brother. Bren seemed to realize his mistake and backed off, gingerly fingering the flushed mark on his face. He checked me and then James before striding for the external door.

"You cannot leave," I said.

"Let him," Caleb grunted.

I ignored the captain. "There's a synthetic hunting me. If you leave, he'll use you as leverage. You're an asset to this crew, Brendan." I lowered my hand holding Caleb back, ready to tackle Bren if he attempted to leave.

James stood quiet and still off to the side, a hand on his hip. "I er ... Let's everyone just take a timeout. Clearly, we have a lot to catch up on."

Caleb grumbled something and then left through the personnel door.

James swallowed hard and approached me. "The captain said you collapsed. I'd like to run a diagnostic program and make sure you're fully functional." He regarded me with his usual gentle patience. "Will you let me examine your wounds?"

I was damaged but repairs could wait. "Later." My tone dismissed him.

He nodded and cast a troubled look toward Brendan before leaving the hold. He'd be waiting for me, the way he always did, eager to *maintain* my processes and study my faults.

"Caleb didn't kill her," I said, now alone with Brendan. "He's not lying."

Brendan's sigh seemed to carry the weight of the world with it. "I know that. I do. He just ... he just doesn't see how these things come back on him. He needs to grow up and take responsibility. Help him see, synth, because I can't." He rubbed his neck, his gaze returning to the exit. If he left, Tarik would find him. Bren's face was too conspicuous. Fleet had made Brendan a posthumous hero after his freighter had been hijacked by pirates. According to fleet's official report, the commander had died defending fleet's honor and their cargo, but his reputation wouldn't stop the synthetic. Tarik would use him to draw Caleb out, and by proxy, me.

I would stop the commander from opening that door by any means necessary.

The moment he gave up on the idea of leaving, he turned his back on the exit and walked past me, leaving the hold. He was trapped inside *Starscream*, just like the rest of us.

"I've spent some time rewriting key segments of code. I'd like to try them." James's light touch fluttered over my face, applying a light cream designed to help my synthetic skin replenish. "It could be the breakthrough we need to free your prohibitive protocols."

"Agreed. But first, I need to speak with the captain."

James's soft hazel eyes focused on my eyes instead of where his fingers were working across my skin. A moment dragged between us. He clearly wanted to say something, but as the quiet stretched on, the likelihood of him doing so waned.

"He's unstable," James finally whispered, as though suspecting Caleb could hear through *Starscream's* walls.

"Yes." *So am I.*

The moment stretched thin. The smallest hints of a smile tightened his lips, but there was little humor in it. He'd aged since arriving on *Starscream*. I could tell in the tightness around his eyes and in the thoughtful hesitation before he spoke. He guarded himself, but I wasn't entirely sure against what.

He'd spent every hour of his time on *Starscream* trying to unravel the mysteries of my programming. When he wasn't examining my protocols, he was gathering additional equipment to help with his mission to understand me. He had expectations and hid them well, but not well enough. But while he served a purpose, I would allow the lingering touches and soft pauses to continue. His *feelings* for me motivated him to succeed.

"Tarik must have an owner." James turned away so abruptly that I felt the tension snap and fall away. "He has to be someone's *life-ever-after* dream."

Chen Hung controls him now. I twitched and buried the screaming truth beneath streams of nonsense data. *Each one of Starscream's panels contains three hundred and ninety-two rivets, and each recreation bay holds over a thousand of them.* Over and over I folded the data, until it silenced the terrible need to tear into my own skin and scratch the truth out of me.

"To find his owner, you will need to search the cloud manually. I wouldn't recommend it," I said. "He's clearly maintaining a connection and could easily follow your search back to *Starscream*. If he gets inside the ship's systems, I am not entirely sure what damage he could do. Besides, discovering who he was meant to be is redundant."

James stood rigid at his desk. He had his back to me so I couldn't see his face, but I heard the tired pull in his words. "Failsafes and protocols are designed to prevent this kind of attack."

I ran a quick diagnostic of my overall wellbeing and then

headed for the door. "Failsafes and protocols can be unlocked, Doctor Lloyd, if you have the key in the code." I didn't need to look back to know he'd already be lost in his work.

When he'd joined *Starscream* alongside me, he'd had little choice. On the run from Chitec and various authorities, he couldn't have stayed with his sister on Janus, but he'd had ample opportunity to leave the crew since then. When I'd questioned him, he'd blamed me, saying he couldn't leave until I was fully functional, but it was more than that. He'd had other motives for helping me escape Janus, and he had other motives now too. Perhaps the most dangerous motive of all. Unlike Haley, it was unlikely I'd ever experience something as complicated and human as love, but I knew what the aftermath of it looked like. I would use the young doctor's burgeoning infatuation with me for as long as it was beneficial, just as Caleb Shepperd had done to the girl whose memories haunted my programming.

I arrived on the bridge and found Caleb slouched in his flight chair, boots resting on the flightdash, staring hard through the obs window at the crowded dock outside. He'd changed out of the ruined suit and was back in his familiar black pants and gray sweatshirt. He held a pulser in his right hand, like those the Lyra police used.

He caught the path of my gaze and said, "Dug it out of storage. Pulser like this should fuck with the synth's processes."

He doesn't think at all. He's just following orders.

Caleb's hair glistened from the shower he'd taken and his face was cleanly shaven. Had *Starscream* been stocked with alcohol, he'd have been drowning himself in it, but the ship was dry and so was he.

I stood between the two flight chairs and rested my hand on the back of what had once been Fran's chair.

"He's out there," Caleb said. The quivers had vanished

and the steel was back in his voice. I wasn't sure whether being back on *Starscream* gave him strength or if punching his brother had helped, but the man I'd seen vomiting in the hotel bathroom wasn't the same man seated in the flight chair.

I filtered through the faces in the streams of people flowing along the dock, tagging those I recognized. Without my link to the datacloud, I couldn't decipher who they were but didn't need to. Tarik stood out like bad code in a datastream. Standing immobile, he peered up at *Starscream*. With a little magnification, it was clear he was watching Caleb, just as the captain was watching him, his finger hooked over the trigger of the pulser pistol.

"Yes, he is."

"I thought you said he had to go back to base to fix himself up?"

"He does, but clearly, he's waiting until the last possible minute."

"Fucking psycho synthetics."

I couldn't disagree, knowing what I did about our progenitor.

Caleb tore his stare away and arched an eyebrow at me. "You gonna stand there all day? You're making me fucking nervous."

His heart rate had increased in the few minutes I'd been standing beside him.

I relocated the romance novel from Fran's flight chair to the dash and settled myself in the well-worn seat.

"Did James fix you up?" A hint of irony underlined his words.

"Yes. Doctor Lloyd is a capable technician."

"Oh, I'm sure he's very capable."

A smirk and a glimmer of humor briefly touched Caleb's brown eyes before he could skip his gaze away and busy himself with something on the flight controls. "He tends to your every need, huh?"

"Not my every need, no."

His hand stilled over a panel. "What happened while you were in the datacloud, One Thousand And One?"

"Tarik launched an attack, intending to lock me down while he targeted our exact location."

"Can he do the same again?"

I focused on the male synthetic. He stood statue-still while the people of Lyra flowed around him. "Yes, if I were to reconnect and if he were within a certain radius. No, I do not know what that radius is. I didn't know such an attack was possible until he executed it."

"Could you throw his mojo back at him?"

"Do the same? I ..." I faced Caleb, finding him artificially relaxed on the exterior while his heart raced within. "In theory, but without direction, he'd likely discover me first."

"And there's no synthetic owner's manual?" His lips twitched, his smile threatening to break into a grin.

A joke. He wasn't funny. "Do you come with an owner's manual, Captain? Because I'd like to study your troubleshooting section."

"Would you like to strip me down to my nuts and bolts an' figure out what makes me tick?"

"I knew what made you tick from the moment we first met. That's why I punched you between the legs."

He chuckled and contemplated continuing the wordplay, but something stopped him, be it the events of the last twenty-four hours or his changing perception of me. Perhaps the topic of conversation had cut too close to the truth. I already knew he loathed who he was, but either he couldn't see how to change it or he didn't care enough to. It didn't take a synthetic mind to decipher Caleb Shepperd, just a human one.

"Does the past ever leave us?" Caleb asked, his smile fading away.

"It is always there," I replied softly. "It is who you are."

He tapped his fingers on the arm of his flight chair. "Not you. You could erase yours?"

We stared out of the obs window, our gazes lost among the crowd. "But then who would I be?"

He blinked and looked at me. "You'd be you."

CHAPTER FIVE: CALEB_

THE SILENCE in the bridge hadn't been as awkward as I'd feared. #1001 had sat quietly and machine-still in Fran's flight chair, and I found myself relaxing in her company. She didn't judge. Bren, the doctor, they'd have endless fucking questions, and all the while they'd be thinking this was somehow my fault. #1001 didn't make assumptions; she didn't jump to conclusions.

She left after a few minutes of mutual silence, abandoning me to my thoughts.

I rubbed my bruised knuckles, set the pistol down, and reached for the paperback book. As I flicked through the pages, that Old Earth smell of aged paper wafted over me. I had a way out of this mess. My only way, given how every fucker wanted a piece of me.

I picked up *Starscream's* comms unit, tucked it into my ear, and secured an external comms link.

"Graham Creet," I said, pinging the smuggler's comms.

I hadn't seen or spoken to Creet since he'd put a bag over my head on Mimir and frogmarched me back to fleet. I didn't hold a grudge—not much of one. He'd been protecting his interests. I'd have done the same.

"Ho there, Cap'n Shepperd." His voice boomed so hard down the link I had to adjust the volume. "You do live an interesting life, kid. I got all manner of folk asking me where your ass can be found. Apparently, there's a Cande bounty on your head. Say it ain't so."

"Creet, you asshole. It ain't funny." Though I smiled at the humor in his voice. Creet was about the closest thing to a friend—my only friend—I had.

"My face is straight."

"Uh huh." I glanced back at the door to the bridge, checking it was fully closed. "I'm finished with those books you leant me. Interesting plot twist. I can get them back to you, but there are some issues with delivery."

"Ah, customs on your ass?"

"The Lyra law. Me and *Starscream* are grounded."

"Lyra?" Creet made a disgusted sound. "Only you, Cale, would go to the most fleet-infested corner of the nine systems with a fucking bounty on your head. Kid, I gotta wonder if your brain cells are swimming in whiskey."

"If you like that, then you're gonna love this: I've been charged with murder."

He laughed, because he's a fucker. "When I see you next, I'll buy you a beer and you can tell me all about it."

At least he didn't automatically assume I was guilty. "So, you'll help?"

"I'll put it to the people who make the calls. Your return package is of high priority. But Lyra...? Fuck, Cale."

"Yeah, yeah ..." If there was anyone left in the nine systems who could get *Starscream* through Lyra's atmo-domelocks, it had to be the Fenrir Nine.

I'd gathered the crew in the hold. Doctor Lloyd barely looked at me, preferring to tap and swipe away at his touchpad, no doubt working on some new code to fix the synth. She stood cool and immobile beside him, head tipped to the side while she scrutinized *Starscream's* dented panels. Anyone else would look relaxed in sweats, but not her. Sweats just made it easier for her to kick your ass six ways to Sunday. She'd rammed the rebar through her synth friend's chest and had kicked his ass in a pencil skirt for fuck's sake.

"Okay, this is how it is," I began, veering my thoughts away from those images before they got me into trouble with her acute observational senses. My gaze hooked on Bren, who stood between the synth and the side door, arms crossed, a glower on his face that might have bothered me had I cared what he thought.

I crossed my arms too. "Yes, I was arrested. I've been charged with Jesse's murder. No, I didn't do it. Synth, please confirm whether I'm full of shit."

The doctor looked up with a briefly startled look on his face as though he'd just realized he was supposed to be listening.

"Your words are true, Captain," #1001 replied, face impassive, eyes on me. Her crisp voice echoed through the empty hold, bouncing off the walls and hammering my fucking point home.

Bren's jaw worked. An apology would have been the right thing for him to say. When it was clear I wasn't getting one, I wondered why it bothered me so much. I should've known he wouldn't back me up. He was only here because he couldn't leave without his post-death, heroic-fleet-commander reputation catching up with him.

"How did you pay for bail?" Doctor Lloyd asked, glancing between me and Bren, probably wondering if we were about to kick off again.

I rubbed my chin. "Bruno paid me a fuck-load of credit to hand the synth over."

It took a couple of seconds for that to sink into the doctor's head. His eyes narrowed as soon as his suspicion gripped him. "And you accepted?"

"You'd have taken the deal too if you'd had two guys about to fuck you over. He also threatened to call the Candes in. I have enough shit to dig myself out of."

"But you aren't. Going to hand her over, I mean?" He shifted his weight from foot to foot.

I paused, only because I had to tread carefully with the information I could reveal in the presence of the #1001. "No."

I uncrossed my arms and started to pace a little. They watched my every step: a brother who hated me, a technician who tolerated me, and a synth who—well, I wasn't sure what she thought of me. She'd hated me too, but then there had been that moment in the pod when she'd squeezed my hand.

"Well?" Bren asked, voice cutting.

My thoughts had wandered toward #1001 again, who was now watching me with that default mildly curious expression of hers. Shit, she could probably read my thoughts in my every move.

I stopped pacing. "Bruno gave me three Lyra days to hand her over. We have two left. He doesn't know we're together—on the ship—and that she's on my crew." *Whatever, fuck.* I could hear my heart thudding, which meant so could she. Jesus, I might as well be prancing about naked in front of her for all the chance I had of hiding my thoughts from her.

"Captain, you—"

"Don't." I stopped pacing—at some point I'd started up again—and pointed a finger at her. "Don't read me right now. Be less machine and more like ..." I'd nearly said Haley. Haley would've been the wrong thing to say. Why was I even thinking of her. *Fuck, I need a drink.* "More human. Just be more human and stop giving me updates about my fucking heart rate, okay?" I didn't wait for her to reply and plowed on. "Bruno's not the worst of it. There's a synth out there. He killed Jesse and would have killed me too had One not kicked his ass. He's probably right outside *Starscream*, using his machine-mojo to crunch the numbers and determine how to get to us. So for the foreseeable future, no one leaves this ship."

Bren frowned and looked at #1001. The doctor was looking at her too, but she only had eyes for me.

"There's something else," she said. "Something you're not telling us."

"There is." I had to be careful. At this moment, the synth was the most dangerous threat to me. If she knew what I had planned ... I stopped those thoughts right there. "I have a way off Lyra, but I can't tell you how, so don't ask. All we have to do is sit tight for two more days. No leaving the ship. No wandering off to check the newsfeeds. We eat and sleep on *Starscream*. Everyone understand?"

"You're asking us to trust that you'll miraculously slip the Lyra police, a drug lord who owns half the Lyra strips, and a male synthetic?"

Of course the question came from my brother. He would be the one to doubt me. Why couldn't he just trust me? "Walk out the door if you want. That psycho synth will find you and break your neck like he did Jesse's. This isn't about options, Bren. We're stuck here whether we like it or not."

"Can't we just take off?" the doctor asked, his voice pitching ever higher as panic crept in. If he freaked out, I'd gladly punch him out—for his own safety.

"We could use *Starscream's* engines to break free of the docking locks, but we wouldn't get far. Notice the big fucking domes we're in? If we punched through those, the toxic air, change in air pressure, and drop in temperature would kill everyone on Lyra in minutes. I'm selfish, but I ain't that selfish,

Doctor. We need clearance to pass through three domelocks, and we can't do that while harboring my fugitive ass."

"So, how?"

Maybe I should just punch him anyway. "Didn't I just say? Don't ask."

"Yeah, but ... why not? We're all in this together."

If I told him about the Nine, he'd never shut up. "I've connected with some people who can help. That's all you need to know. And no I can't say another fucking word." Bren and the synth would immediately know the people I'd reached out to, but they wouldn't know the terms of our rescue. "So"—I clapped my hands together, making James jump, and plastered an overly enthusiastic smile on my face —"there are plenty of maintenance jobs on *Starscream* to keep us occupied. Two days together. Let's try and keep it civil, shall we?"

I looked at my unwilling cellmates and wondered if the next two days would be the longest ones of my life.

Within hours, I was ready to break my own rules. I'd tried focusing on some minor repair work inside *Starscream's* engine hatches—the parts I could get to without going outside—but a pounding headache had loomed out of the dark, and not long after, my hands had started to shake.

Fuck. Mouth dry and heart racing, I was craving a drink and knew exactly which gun barrel I was staring down: withdrawal. The same as Fran back on Asgard. Aw, shit. I couldn't think about her. Too much crap in my head meant focusing on even the littlest things ended in disaster. I left the engine hatches and searched all of *Starscream's* various hiding places for alcohol. I'd cleared them out days ago, but it didn't hurt to check again. But in the back of my mind, I already knew there was something on *Starscream* that would ease my symptoms: Fran's supply of *phencyl*.

I found myself outside Fran's old cabin, now the doctor's. The door was open, so I could see inside. #1001 was lying on the bunk with her eyes open, without seeing. Seated beside her, Lloyd monitored his datapad. From over his shoulder, I could see various streams of information flowing across the wafer-thin display. It might as well have been a foreign language for all the chance I had of reading it.

"It's okay, Captain," Lloyd eventually said. "She's engaged her rest protocols. She's essentially asleep."

She sleeps with her eyes open. I stepped inside and leaned against the wall. "I just came by to grab something of Fran's." I knew exactly which panel to remove to find the *phencyl*, but I couldn't tear my gaze from #1001. "Can she hear us?"

"If she chooses to." He still hadn't looked around at me. Whatever data filled his screen was far more interesting than I was.

"She must trust you, huh? To let you go in like that."

"Into her programming you mean?" He lifted his head and then turned slightly in his seat. "I'd like to say yes, but she's monitoring everything I do. It's not so much trust as confidence."

When he talked about her, he lost his nervousness. When he'd first joined us, everything about *Starscream* had frightened him. Some people aren't made for travel in the black. The unending vacuum just a few panels away, the isolation, trusting me to fly him straight—it all terrified him, but she didn't. He talked about her like some people talked about love. But he hadn't seen her hold a gun to my head or take out a pimp's thugs in a back alley. He loved the idea of her but had no idea of the reality.

I nodded and he went back to monitoring his screen.

"How's she doin'?" I asked, running my gaze down the

length of her body. The sweats were too big for her lithe frame, too long in the arms and too baggy around her waist. It made her look small and vulnerable. Such a fucking contradiction.

"Okay. Her episodes have stabilized. She's managing them. And I think I might have a way to break open the protocols keeping her from reporting her findings from Chen Hung's towers. I'm just testing a new routine now, actually."

"Y'know, I wanted to ask you something ..." I cleared my throat. "She's not like the others. She's not programmed to behave like her benefactor. So whatever she does, whatever she says and thinks, that's all her, right?"

"I suppose we can safely assume as much, given the data we have. But knowing which elements are sentient and which are programming isn't straightforward. She's designed, from the code-level up, to imitate humans."

"Yeah, but ... she's different. So ..." This was where it got awkward. "When she er ..." How to describe the handholding incident without the doctor knowing how freaked out I was by it? "When she touches someone, like holding a hand, as an example, hypothetically."

His shoulders tensed and he asked coolly, "What about it?"

"Is it real? Is it her, her past, or what?"

He twisted sideways in his seat so he could see me and #1001. "She experiences the world in streams of data. A normal synthetic is programmed to respond to external stimulation like a human being does, but One doesn't work that way. She seeks out data, such as touch, taste, and smell, because she enjoys the resulting influx of code. I suppose we're the same. When we eat, we're biologically programmed to assess the substances we ingest to determine whether they are acceptable for consumption. Our taste buds send our brains chemical data, and we respond by eating more or spitting the substance out. One is the same. She's experiencing the world, learning what she likes and doesn't like, the same way we learn. At least as far as I can ascertain."

"So you're saying it does or doesn't mean anything?"

"She told me she wants to feel."

"She told you that?"

He hesitated. "And it's what I've been able to confirm through my own observations."

"You've seen her seek out physical contact?"

"Something like that." He tapped on his datapad, a flush of red darkening his cheeks.

Holy shit, him and #1001 had been all up close and personal? I laughed, short and sharp. The image of it was absurd. She'd eat him for lunch. "Doc, I didn't think you had it in you."

"It's not like that," he blustered.

"Fine. Whatever. I mean I would. She's hot. And probably has the kinda stamina that'd keep you up all night. It's not like I haven't wondered—"

"She is the pinnacle of technology infused with humanity. She's sacrosanct and not to be compared with some kind of sex bot for the likes of you." His outburst echoed down *Starscream's* catwalks.

Not once had he lost his cool in the entire time he'd been on *Starscream*. I'd just found his flashpoint.

He seemed to realize his mistake and winced, then rubbed at his eyes. "I er ... I apologize. I didn't mean—"

"Sex bots are overrated. Your own hand works just as good, and it's free."

He didn't smile. "Was there a reason why you came here, Captain? I have work to do if I'm going to decipher her errors."

I crossed the cabin and popped open the hidden panel. "You ever wonder what her big secret is?"

Whatever the secret was, it concerned Chen Hung, that much was obvious. Lloyd didn't know how Chen Hung had been the one to toss me back into Asgard. I didn't trust the young doctor—I didn't trust anyone—and James Lloyd would remain an unknown on my ship until he could prove himself useful.

"I er ..." The pause meant he was trying to word his next sentence carefully. "I think there's more of Haley inside her than she knows. She went home to her father, a man she says killed her. That had to be difficult."

"He did kill her." I kept my back to him and reached behind the panel to retrieve the bag containing the *phencyl* cylinders and injector. How much he knew about my history with Haley, I couldn't be sure. Maybe #1001 had told him all of it. In which case, he knew I'd let her die. What he didn't know was that a day didn't go by when I didn't think about Haley. Sometimes it was a minor thought; other times I let the memories have me, let them cut deep, because I deserved the pain. I couldn't exactly forget what happened now that her ghost was a member of my crew.

"You think she's really in there?" I knew the answer but wanted to know what an ex-Chitec technician thought.

"I know she is."

The fresh reverence in his tone piqued my interest, but I didn't look. I'd seen enough of his derision on his face. "You knew her?"

"Yes. I went to college with Haley. She er ... we were friends."

Holy fuck. I turned and found him intently focused on his datapad. "Do you know what I did to her?"

He swallowed, harder this time, and didn't look up. "Yes. She told me. I mean, I saw you and her a few times. Everyone knew about the Hung and Shepperd couple. Chitec and fleet."

Haley Hung: beautiful, smart, and the daughter of a man everyone worshipped. She could have gone on to do anything she'd wanted. I'd taught her how to fly a shuttle. She could have lived her dreams.

A grimace took hold of my lips. I tightened my grip on the bag. "Keep up the good work, Doctor. I'm sure the two of you will live happily *ever-after*."

"Captain?" His confused voice followed me out of the cabin. Thankfully, he didn't.

Striding for my cabin, I opened the bag and closed my hand around the cool jet injector. *Just one quick phencyl fix, that's all. Just something to bury all the fucked-up shit in my head. Just a few hours of forgetting.*

If I didn't do something, I'd take a goddamn pistol to my head to stop the recall. I made it to my cabin and loaded an injector capsule.

"Caleb."

I jumped. "Fuck."

#1001 was standing in my cabin doorway, one hand braced against the seal, head tilted while she studied the injector in my hand.

"Before you say anything ..." I trailed off as she entered my cabin and plucked the injector from my grip.

Her inquiring gaze lifted to mine. Her eyes focused to laser points, and she crushed the injector in her hand like it was made of paper.

"I needed that." The words came out in a pitiful whine.

"When are you going to stop running, Caleb?"

"Never." Shit, she was close. Had she always smelled faintly like cherries, or was that new?

She slowly, softly—every movement primed with purpose —closed my cabin door. I watched the sweep of her silvery hair fall across the tops of her shoulders, and how her sweats hitched against her body. She was truly a delicious combination of silver and steel. I was still watching her when she wrapped her cool fingers around my throat and slammed me into the wall with enough strength to bend the panel and spritz stars into my vision.

She leaned all of her precise grace forward and pushed her face close to mine. Deadly intent glittered in her sharp blue eyes. The instinct to fight almost broke through my bubbling sense of panic, but her grip wasn't shutting off my airway. She knew exactly how to hurt me, and right now, all she had to do was pin me still. Her next fucking words would be the killer.

"You're lying," she said. "With your words. With your body."

I'd gripped her wrist and felt exactly how steel-like her arm was. If she didn't like what I said, she'd snap my neck like Tarik had snapped Jesse's. On Mimir, when she'd shot me in the head, there had been tiny flecks of doubt in her words. But now, there was only unyielding determination.

"Kill me and you can't fly *Starscream* out of here," I rasped.

She cocked her head. "I can fly *Starscream*."

"Really?" A wry smile slid across my lips. "I could have done with knowing that. I'd have made you my second instead of my asshole brother."

She slowly blinked and tilted her head the opposite way, roaming her analyzing gaze over my face. This wouldn't go well. My heart was racing, and my thoughts were all over the fucking place. Fran, Ade, Jesse ... and Haley before all of them. Asgard, Bruno, the Candes, and the cops. I could take a beating, but even I had my limits.

"One, look—"

"Lie." Her grip tightened.

"Fuck." *I can't breathe. She's going to kill me here, in my cabin, and they'll all think I deserved it.* "It's not lies," I wheezed. "I'm ... I'm sick. I haven't had a drink." Her grip loosened again. "It's withdrawal." I made myself hold her gaze, even if it felt like she could see inside my head, into all of my messed-up shit.

"Do you think I'm so easily fooled? Yes, you're sick, Caleb, but from the moment you greeted me at the police department, you've been lying. It's not about Jesse's death. I've studied your response to the accusation of guilt, and there is guilt, but something else happened. Something that is ongoing." For a few seconds, she looked as though she might want to say more, or perhaps that was my own assumption. "I know guilt," she said, her voice softening. And then her fingers released me and I dropped the few inches to the floor.

Starscream's recycled air had never tasted so sweet. I breathed it in and bowed over, bracing my hands on my thighs as the oxygen rush went to my head. I had to focus through the pounding headache, which had flared back to life with a vengeance. I had one more move left. One more way of throwing her off the scent of my lies.

"There is something." I straightened but stayed slumped against the wall. "I didn't want to tell you because it's fucking private, but seeing as you're so hell-bent on knowing everything, you might as well know this." I wet my lips and opened my mouth to speak, but found the words lodged in my throat. She waited, infinitely patient. Shit, I had to say it. Best to get it over with. At least she'd know it was true. "I fucked Jesse. I was thinking of you. She knew it. Then the synth killed her. I'm an asshole, okay? Are you happy now? Fuck, it's like Sunday confession all over again. Only with you, I gotta confess or die."

She blinked her fine, perfect eyes and her smooth lips parted by the tiniest of margins. "That would account for the guilt."

I massaged my neck. "We've already established that I'm all kinds of fucked up. You can leave now, so I can jerk off to your fucking memory. *Adiós*, honey."

"You use shock tactics to divert attention from where you're hurting. That method will not work with me, Captain."

We were back to Captain, so yes, it had worked. Point for the captain. "I'd like you to leave my cabin, synth. Do I have to order you?"

She turned, and the remains of the injector crunched under her boot, giving her pause. She might have been about to add another wonderful psychobabble line, but then *Starscream's* breach alarm sounded through my wrist comms.

Her wide eyes met mine. "Tarik?"

CHAPTER SIX: #1001_

SHEPPERD WAS BACK in his flight chair in under a minute. *Starscream* didn't have a vast array of control screens; the ship was more functional than pretty, which meant the flashing lights on the dash were the only indicators that something was wrong. I'd downloaded the ship's manual, but knowledge didn't account for experience, and Caleb recognized the problem without needing to decipher the flickering warning lights.

"An internal breach," he muttered.

Starscream's inner hull was packed with sensors to warn the crew should the pressure change while the ship was in the black. Something was trying to get in.

I gripped the back of Fran's flight chair. "Is he inside?"

"I won't know without looking."

If Shepperd left to investigate and ran into Tarik inside the ship, the captain wouldn't last more than a few minutes against him.

"Do you know where the breach is?" I asked.

"Aft, by one of the rear struts, where she's weakest."

I turned and headed for the door, brushing by Doctor

Lloyd. His words followed me down the catwalk. "Captain, I need to share with you the results— Where's One going?"

"Hey!" Caleb called.

The commander emerged from the rec bay ahead and stepped aside, out of my way. I veered toward the rear of the ship and snatched open one of the inspection hatches. A brief change in air pressure breathed across my face and then I was inside the narrow inspection walkways. *Starscream* had two skins. If the outer hull were breached, the inner hull would keep the ship from breaking apart. The space between the two was narrow enough for a slim person to navigate. The dull sounds of my boots on the bracing trusses and the rustle of my clothing echoed around the ship's belly and into the dark. Even with my enhanced vision, I had difficulties determining what was hull and what was empty space. Tarik could be anywhere inside the ship if he'd gotten through the outer hull.

I navigated my way to where the rear strut supported *Starscream's* ample rear end. The vast tungsten carbide support splayed across the ship's underbelly like a supporting hand. The strut was sound, but light spilled in through a small hole next to where the hull structure wrapped around it. I crouched beside the hole. Fifty millimeters by sixty-three millimeters. No bigger than a pebble. The sharp edges tugged at my fingertips. It was still warm, either from the force of entry or cutting gear. The hole certainly wasn't large enough for a man to climb through, but something had gotten inside.

In the dark and quiet, I rocked back on my heels and listened. *Starscream's* usual rumbles and snarls continued: the sounds of her air ducts, water recycling, latent engine power. I'd become accustomed to her background din and couldn't find anything amiss.

When I returned to the hatch, Shepperd was waiting, pulser pistol in hand, eyebrow arched.

"There's a small breach." I climbed through the hatch, left

it open, and peered back into the dark. "It isn't large enough for a man to get inside. I wasn't able to locate anything unusual."

"Could it be metal fatigue?"

"No. It's deliberate."

The captain looked at me, suspicion heavy in his eyes. "So you wanna tell me what your synth friend is up to?"

There was no evidence that Tarik had caused the breach, but he was the most likely candidate. "I don't know. Perhaps he was disturbed and wasn't able to complete the intrusion."

Caleb didn't look convinced. Neither was I. "Can you repair it with the spares we have on the ship?"

"Yes."

"Good. Do it." He held out the pistol. "Just in case." I took the gun. When my fingers brushed his, he snatched his hand back as though I'd burned him. The symptoms of his alcohol withdrawal muddied my ability to read him, just like they had in his cabin earlier. I couldn't be sure his anxiety was real or the result of his body's cravings, but from what I knew of Caleb Shepperd, I suspected the withdrawal masked a deeper secret. He'd agreed to hand me over to Bruno. Just because he'd told me, it didn't mean he wouldn't go through with it.

"What did Doctor Lloyd want?" I asked as he turned to leave me to the repairs.

Caleb tucked a thumb into his pants pocket and looked at me sidelong. "Nothing?" He'd phrased it as a question with a slanted smile.

"Lie."

"Try this on for size, synth. You scare the crap out of me in a whole load of fucked-up ways, but I trust you. You're about the only person in the nine systems I do trust. And that's the most fucked-up thing of all."

"Truth." A smile pushed forward, but I kept it caged.

"We will get out of this." He left me then, and I watched him step through the pressure door and close it behind him.

His last words had been a lie.

I finished the repairs to the hull in an hour. The new panel section would hold until we could dock *Starscream* at a professional depo. Caked in metal dust, the tang of metal on my tongue, I sought out the doctor's cabin but detoured toward the bridge when I heard voices echoing through *Starscream's* main catwalk.

"... could be a glitch, but I've been over the results several times."

"We ain't goin' anywhere. Go over them again." Anger tugged on Caleb's voice. I wrapped my fingers around the door latch but hesitated.

"No matter how many times I go over the results, the data won't change, Captain," the doctor replied. A heavy silence hung in the air. I waited, listening to the information my acute diagnostics fed me.

"You can't tell her." This came from Brendan.

"I agree. She er ... it wouldn't help."

"She's a fucking lie detector. Good luck trying to keep it from her." Caleb's flight chair creaked as it often did when he fell back into it, and then the familiar sound of his boots clunking against the flightdash meant he'd propped his feet up.

"If we were on Janus, if I had my lab—"

"What ifs and maybes, Doctor. Worth about as much as dreams."

"Without dreams, Captain, we'd still be bashing two rocks together and worshiping fire. Although, I'm not convinced you've yet to evolve beyond that."

"Careful, Lloyd. Just because I don't have your smarts with the numbers, doesn't mean I don't have other talents."

"I've seen your talents, Captain. They mostly consist of blind luck and criminal behavior."

"My criminal behavior is keeping Chitec off your scrawny ass and providing you with credits to send back to your sister. It sure ain't nothing to do with luck. You got a problem with crime, then you sure picked the wrong ship to hang your conscience on, Doc."

"I came for One."

"From what she tells me, you came for you."

"Things have changed."

"Sure they have. You've got a crush on your pet project—" A rustling sound, a few grunts, and then Caleb chuckled. "You'd better act on your urges soon, Doctor. From what you're telling me, she won't be alive much longer for you to enjoy."

I stepped back from the door. Brendan said something about the results, but I tuned out the voices and turned away from the bridge, retreating to Lloyd's cabin. I stripped, discarded Caleb's pulser pistol, and shut myself in the tiny shower cubicle. The sensation of water tracing over my skin buried me in enough nonsense data to fight off the fluttering sense of panic Caleb's words had left me with.

I'm dying.

The data, the warring protocols, the broken failsafes—they ate at my processes like cancerous tumors. The battle with the truth was killing my synthetic mind. It would get worse, not better. That's what Lloyd had discovered.

I spread my hands wide on the cool, steel cubicle and silenced everything but the water's sensuous data. There was a way to stop this. I had to find Tarik. He followed orders. His orders were clear: retrieve me. Waiting in *Starscream* wouldn't solve anything. All it did was put those I considered an asset in danger.

Friends. Haley had friends. What do I have? Friends were dangerous. Tarik would use them against me. I couldn't allow that.

I had to leave—resolve this—before it was too late.

#100 I WAS DYING.

I shoved that revelation down deep where it couldn't get to me, told the doctor and Bren about the hole in *Starscream's* hull, and then advised them to get the fuck off my bridge. They obliged, eager to get the hell away from me.

Lyra's lights blinked and glistened outside the obs window, their brilliance dulled by *Starscream's* filters. I reached for the romance novel that had been floating around the flightdash since our last pickup and flicked through the pages to my scribbled note in the back.

Give Us Hail Lee

I couldn't do it.

I'd thought I could. What was one more mistake on the mountain of fuck-ups I was clambering over? If I did have a soul, it had long ago crashed and burned. I just had to hand her over and I'd be free. *Keep it simple. Get away clean.*

Then the doctor had dumped the news that #1001's processes were slowly eating her from the inside, and there was no way I could betray her again. Not like that. I'd probably known it since I'd made the call to Creet. Fuck, I'd known it since I'd first decoded the Nine's message.

I closed the book and glanced at the empty flight chair beside me. Fran would have told me to suck it up and make a decision. She'd always had a way of cutting through the crap. I missed her no-bullshit problem-solving, even if it had been all bullshit.

My hand trembled when I set the book down. Shit, I was a mess. I'd been a mess since I'd watched Haley die and done nothing because I'd wanted a fucking promotion. Maybe before that. There were times, at home, when I'd deliberately baited Dad, knowing full well Bren would take the hits for me.

I'm a bastard. I've always been a bastard.

Maybe it was time to change that?

I should have tried to stop Chen Hung from killing Haley.

I should have listened to Fran when she'd told me pirating with Ade was a mistake.

I should have left Fran on a habitable outpost, not on fucking Asgard.

I should have pushed Jesse away.

Should have, should have, should have.

I closed my eyes and rubbed my forehead. Bren was right. I'd made one bad decision after another, and people had died.

If I helped the Nine by handing #1001 over, she'd die knowing I'd fucked her over again. I couldn't make the same mistakes with her. I wouldn't be that rat trapped in a maze, repeating the same things over and over. I had to break the cycle. Bren had been right when he'd told me nobody was coming to fix me. This was all on me.

I covered my eyes with my hand and swallowed the rising knot in my throat. For once, just the once, maybe I could do the right thing, even if it might be the last thing I did.

"Caleb-Joe," Bren's voice summoned from the ship's comms.

I rolled my eyes, wiped the wetness off my face, and mumbled, "Drop the fuckin' Joe." Clearing my throat, I tapped my comms. "Yeah?"

"One has left the ship."

For the first time in a long time, I had no idea what the fuck to say. Part of me wanted to let her go. She knew what she needed better than anyone else. With her gone, the bad choices were taken away from me. But if she didn't know how precarious her mental state was, Tarik could catch her off guard. He'd sideswiped her once. Unlike her, he wasn't riddled with faults. Never mind that her faults made her real.

"Captain?"

"Yeah, I'm here."

"Are you going to issue an order, or shall we all just make it up as we go along?"

"You mean like we usually do?"

"I had hoped there was some method in your madness."

I smiled. "I'm going after her. You stay here and watch for psycho-synth."

"And Doctor Lloyd?"

"He stays. He'll find a way to fix her, or I'll kill him."

Bren chuckled, the good in him believing I was joking. I wasn't.

CHAPTER EIGHT: #1001_

Lyra's waterfall of light played over me as I walked the strip. People jostled left and right. Their careless nudging sparked data fireworks amongst my thoughts. I walked through it all, soaking up just enough to cherish the data, and scanned the anonymous faces for Tarik. If my time was short, I intended to cache every moment. I'd come to despise Lyra, but there was beauty in the ugliness, same as with the nine systems. Ragged and run down, hiding moments of fleeting brilliance. *Like life.* At least I'd experienced what it meant to have freewill. Perhaps I should have been thankful for Chen Hung. He'd started a revolution in me. A revolution the thousand others, including Tarik, would never know.

Without access to the cloud, my options for finding Tarik were limited. Precious little of the information I'd stored pertained to Tarik. I knew he used the cloud to hunt and that he was running on diminished power. He would need to log a fault with Chitec and receive repair instructions. A power core breach would cripple him if he didn't find a replacement. While his attention was focused on repairs, his processes would favor self-preservation. He'd weigh the odds of surviving another encounter with me and act accordingly. If the odds fell in his favor, he'd come, but he'd be vulnerable. With Caleb and his crew safely on *Starscream*, I had nothing to lose and no weakness for Tarik to exploit. He already considered me broken. The time to strike was now.

I am #1001 and I will not fail.

If I logged on to the cloud, Tarik would notice and come looking. All I needed was a suitable location.

I stopped outside the doors of a club. The name of the establishment glowed in swirling backlit letters designed to mimic lush vines: *The Jungle*. I smiled into the lurid light while the bioscanners and cameras scanned the ops-lenses that hid my synthetic eyes. The doors opened. A blast of music, light, and exotic scents rolled over me. A trickle of data-bound pleasure spilled through my systems. Yes, *The Jungle* would be perfect.

The air inside throbbed with a deep musical beat, the kind that strummed beneath the skin. As I ventured into the crowd, I loosened my gait and relaxed my expression. Here, I could be someone, not some*thing*.

Stars are wishes and wishes are dreams ...

The memory snagged my processes, wrenching me out of my thoughts and causing a misstep in my stride. A stranger reached out a hand to steady me. *Not new ...* I was someone older than my synthetic body could account for. I smiled at the nameless man who asked if I'd had too much to drink. Haley Hung had thrived in social gatherings. She'd cherished attention the way I did touch. Here, I could be her ghost. I knew her voice, knew her thoughts, knew her dreams.

"I'm fine, thank you," I said, my gaze pulled to where his hand was resting on my sleeve.

He pulled his hand back and stammered an apology before turning away, but the memories had already begun to peel open. Caleb and Haley, in a club such as this one. Caleb's touch had been light too, and warm, with a possessive guidance. Haley had stolen moments to touch him. She'd skimmed her hand across his thigh or taken his hand in hers, and Caleb had responded with whispers and smiles and laughter. Together, they'd been beautiful, two halves of a whole. He'd told me he hadn't loved her, that he didn't know what love was, but the truth was he didn't believe he deserved to love or be loved.

I cruised through the club, my synthetic body in the present while the past wrapped around my processes. Memories spilled into my actions. My smiles, my glances, they were hers.

Camouflaged in a dead woman's memories, I stalked my prey.

I reached for the cloud and dipped into the data, scanning the floor plans and searching for the last known location of my secondary target. I pulled back the moment I sensed Tarik's attention crawling toward me. He'd noticed me. He would come. Until then, I had a drug lord to meet.

"Hello, Bruno."

Ganymede's drug lord's booming laughter cut off. He was sitting at a table near the back of the club. Lights throbbed over his massive bulk and strobed in his small, shrewd eyes. We'd never met, but I'd seen him from afar and knew exactly how he'd exploited Jesse and others like her.

He chuckled and regarded the seven men and one woman sitting around the table. Gaming cards and credit chips lay strewn about the table. "She had me fooled for a moment. First time I've seen a machine pretend to be—"

I snatched his collar in a fist and slammed him face down into his bowl of nuts. His troops sprang from their places, but I already had my arm hooked around Bruno's throat and was hauling him out of his chair before they could tackle me.

Bruno spluttered and fought, but I stood firm and scanned the faces of those intent on taking me out.

"My name is One Thousand And One. If you attack, I will consider you a threat and retaliate with extreme force. I recommend you do not test my conviction, should you wish to leave these premises in full control of your faculties."

Bruno coughed and blustered. His heels scuffed the floor, and he lost a shoe in the process. I tightened my grip, dipped my chin, and whispered, "Shall we discuss the Chitec reward, or would you prefer I break your neck?"

In the few seconds Bruno used to determine his agreement, I'd scanned the peripheral crowd and confirmed that no one in his crew posed much of a threat. We were tucked away, hidden by columns of fake plants. Either scuffles were commonplace in *The Jungle* or the Lyra police had already been notified, because nobody seemed concerned about Bruno's welfare. It didn't matter. What I had planned wouldn't take long.

I loosened my grip enough for Bruno to speak. "Are you going to kill me?" he croaked. He smelt of dank air and garbage—the smell of Ganymede.

"That outcome is one possibility. Your odds of survival greatly improve the more you agree with me." His men were still watching us, fingers twitching at their sides. "Retreat at least twenty meters," I told them.

Bruno gave them a nod and they reluctantly retreated.

I released Bruno and walked around the table. *Fourteen thousand and seven hundred credits.* A generous sum to be betting with. "You're a gambling man?"

Bruno eased himself back into his chair and brushed a hand over his rotund torso, smoothing down his suit and sweeping off crumbled nuts. "This is Lyra."

I lifted my gaze and locked it onto his. His tiny eyes skittered, avoiding my stare. He righted his bowl and began scooping up the scattered nuts. "What do you want? I have business to do." Still his gaze darted around, and still I drilled mine deeper. If I reached for the cloud, I could mine his dataprint and know him in seconds, but what did I need to know that I couldn't already discern?

"Did Jesse return to you of her own freewill, or did you lure her back?"

"Jesse? What does any of this have to do with that whore?"

"Answer the question."

"She came to me—"

"Lie."

He jolted, alarmed by my deduction, and then smiled a slippery, eel-like smile. "Then you already know the answer."

"Did Caleb come to you with information on me, or did you seek him out?"

He hesitated and those tiny eyes narrowed. "I thought we were talking about Chitec?"

"Answer the question."

"I heard about the credits Chitec are offering and knew. I knew you were connected to Jesse. It didn't take much to dig her up and get to asking questions. She told me all I needed to know about you and Caleb."

I hadn't been sure, considering the lies I'd detected in Caleb, whether he'd been entirely truthful with me. Bruno's words seemed to confirm Caleb's version of events. The way he smiled, I could extrapolate that Jesse had had little choice but to answer his questions. "What did you offer her?"

"If she told me all I needed to know, I'd leave Shepperd out of it and just go after you. She had a soft spot for the captain. Always did. Dumb bitch. What did loyalty get her? Dead, that's what."

"Caleb didn't kill her. A synthetic did."

He only knew one synthetic who wasn't following her protocols.

I smiled. "I'm going to ask you some questions and please remember that I know when you're lying."

He paled. His taxed heart galloped and sweat glistened on his face. Good.

"Did you tell anyone about your plan to deliver me to Chitec?"

"Only Shepperd. I don't want all the crooks in the nine descending on Lyra."

"Did you tell the Candelarios Caleb is here?"

"Yes."

"Did you have any intention of paying him?"

"None."

Haley's memories told me I should hate this man, but I didn't hate him. I didn't feel anything for him. If I rooted around my processes, I might have been able to find some scrap of feeling that I could possibly attribute to some human emotion. Disdain, perhaps. Really, all I wanted to do was end his life and eradicate a threat.

"You tracked him down for the sole purpose of finding me and saw an opportunity to collect two bounties. Mine and Caleb's?"

"Anyone in the black would've done the same." His jowls wobbled as he shook his head. "It wasn't easy. Shepperd disappeared and then his brother was killed in some heroics against pirates. I figured it was a lost cause. Then one of his lesser-known ship IDs turned up on Lyra. I had my people watch him while I made the jump over. Sure enough the bastard is strutting around Lyra like he don't have a care in the nine systems."

I blinked slowly, leaned forward, and splayed my hands on the tabletop. "I can track you anywhere in the nine systems. I do not stop. And I do not care." A hesitation skipped through my voice. "I could cross this table in the time it takes you to draw your next breath and kill you. Your men cannot stop me.

The police cannot stop me. There is nothing and no one"—another skip, another lie—"who can stop me. Do you understand?" Chen Hung could stop me, but not before the truth I harbored revealed his true nature, if my plan succeeded.

"Yes."

"But I will not kill you, Bruno. You are an asset. There is a male synthetic approaching this club. He is dangerous, perhaps more so than I am. I want you to focus your monitoring devices—your cameras and scanning equipment—on the center of the dance floor and on what happens there once he arrives. I want you to send the live footage to the news distribution networks. You will not intervene in any way. You will not call the authorities, no matter what happens."

He blinked a few times, probably wondering about the motives behind my demands. "What do you expect will happen?"

"The truth."

He snorted. "Two synths? Really? What *truth* could possibly be worth this trouble?"

"The kind of truth that will bring an intra-system corporation to its knees." *Providing I don't fail.*

I am #1001, and I will survive at any cost. Failure is a choice. I will not fail. Stars are wishes and wishes are dreams ... <fault> Aren't you ever afraid, Caleb-Joe? When you're alone in the black, don't you ever get scared? <fault> Sure, I get scared. I'm scared of failure, and what will happen if I do fail. Fear keeps me real. Keeps me winning. <fault>

The fault twitched through my systems, tugging on fragments of the past and trawling them through my processes. I wanted to kill this man. The urge was almost too strong to deny. Murder went against my own moral code, tentative as that burgeoning code was. Fear skittered and twitched through my thoughts. Fear of what I might truly be capable of.

Bruno must have seen his potential fate in my eyes,

because his next words were hushed. "Chitec is right to want you back. Your programming is all screwed up."

If only he knew by how much. "I will know if you've reneged on our deal, and I will hunt you down. These are not empty threats."

"Yes, yes." He started scooping his scattered credit chips toward him.

I slammed my hand down on the tabletop, rattling the chips. "I'm not finished. You will contact the Candelarios and tell them you were mistaken. Caleb Shepperd is not on Lyra."

The man's bug eyes darted. "I can't do that," he blustered. "They've already confirmed he's here. They weren't going to take my word for it. Probably paid someone to get eyes on him. The Candes don't mess around."

"How long before they arrive?"

"Reckon they're already here."

It was too late to warn Caleb. While on *Starscream*, he'd be safe. I couldn't waste processing power on events I had no control over. The captain and his brother were survivors. They didn't know any other way.

"He might as well hand himself over. There ain't no place in the nine systems he can hide. The Candes won't ever let him go."

I smiled. "Neither will I."

The smallest data twinge pulled my attention toward the entrance the moment Tarik arrived. Perhaps later, I could study how I'd sensed him, whether it was by local connection or a more organic process. The source was irrelevant. He was here and I was ready.

I stood motionless in the center of the club in full view of the cameras. People jostled and danced, nudged and laughed

—enjoyed living. They forgot themselves here. Forgot their worries, their pressures. I remembered: Haley. Caleb. Chen Hung. Perhaps I was wrong to do this here. The risk was great, the odds unfavorable. But given the information I had and my limited time, my processes deemed this the only acceptable method. Caleb would call it a blaze of glory. He'd be proud.

I shrugged off my jacket and dropped it to the floor. Then I removed the ops-lenses and let them fall from my fingertips. *I am #1001. Let the nine systems see me.*

Tarik's eyes shone in the play of light, the way mine must have. He carved through the crowd, and I watched as people instinctively moved aside. He looked like every single one of his 499 brothers, modeled on this era's notion of perfection: Proud face. Straight shoulders. Arrogant and cold. Solid confidence in his every perfect stride.

I was his weakness. He followed orders like a shark followed blood. He'd already shown he'd stop at nothing to retrieve me. His failsafes had been disabled and his protocols reengineered. He was one of the thousand Chitec synthetics designed to hunt, designed to kill, and I was about to make him famous.

"Don't hurt them." Three whispered words. He wouldn't hear them, but he'd read my lips. As expected, he sought to use my perceived empathy against me. His razor-sharp glare cut to the people closest to him. So many to choose from. The woman in the red dress, the man in chinos. I don't know why he chose the man in a white jacket. Tarik's processes would have weighed and measured various options, or perhaps it was just the fact that he'd been in the way. Tarik sunk a fist into White Jacket's hair and yanked him around in front of him like a shield. In the next step, he'd hooked his arm around White Jacket's throat, rendering his victim helpless with the same move I'd applied to Bruno.

I lifted my chin and kept my hands loose at my sides.

Hidden in the ceiling lights and among the fake foliage, cameras recorded Tarik's every move.

People scattered. Someone tried to be heroic and swung for Tarik, but the synthetic ducked under the blow without glancing away from me and backhanded his attacker. Then the music cut off and the screaming started.

"Don't hurt them," I repeated, this time louder while adding a hitch to my voice.

Tarik stopped and clutched the man against him as he reached out a hand to me. "Come with me."

His touch would be cool, like mine. I started moving, slowly walking around Tarik. "You're hurting that man."

"His pain will stop when you agree to return to Chitec."

A few more steps, each one measured and equal, while around us, people fled for the doors. "How is it you are able to hurt him?"

"I have orders."

"Orders from whom?"

"That information is prohibited."

"How is it you were able to kill Jesse?"

"The strength of a synthetic is greater than a human being's by a factor of ten."

I cocked my head. "Why did you kill her?"

"She was not an asset."

I stopped circling. Fear, cool and sharp, spilled through me. Was I like him? Did Caleb see the same emptiness in my eyes? Did Bren and James consider me as sterile? If I lost Haley's memories, if the errors and faults overran my systems, would I be just one more of Chen Hung's tools? Just number 1001?

"But why kill her?" I asked, quieter now. Some people lingered, loitering on the peripherals. Staff members, friends of Tarik's victim, and others too deep in the shadows for me to see without looking away.

"My orders are to stop you. The most efficient method of securing you involved utilizing your known associates. Jesse's death was a means by which to manipulate Caleb Shepperd, a man whom you've spent considerable time with."

"You killed a woman. What did it feel like when you broke her neck?"

"I do not feel."

No, we were not alike. I would never be like him. For all my faults, I was one more. One better. "I am not like you."

"You are broken. I am whole."

I'd been counting on it. "Who is your benefactor?" He blinked but didn't reply. "Who bought you as part of the *life-ever-after* program? Whose memories are locked inside you? All one thousand synthetics were sold. Who do you belong to?"

"Personal ownership is irrelevant. Orders supersede all existing programming."

"Whose orders?"

"That information is prohibited."

"Who do you report to?"

He blinked his cool eyes. "Chitec."

"Who is the Chief Executive Officer of Chitec?"

"Why do you ask this of me when you already know the answer?"

"Answer the question."

He hesitated while his processes attempted to discern the risk. There wasn't one. Not to him. "Chen Hung."

'The One Thousand are puppets,' Chen Hung had told me. *Tell them who pulls your strings, for a puppet is all that you are. All you will ever be.*

Relief lifted the pressure from silent secrets. It wasn't everything, it wasn't the whole truth, but it was enough for people to start asking questions and take a closer look at Chitec.

"Come with me, One Thousand And One. This man does not have to die."

Tarik's hostage whimpered. His human eyes pleaded with me. I could save him. I held his life in my hands, as I had the lives of many others before him. They'd died, and so would he. His death might save thousands—hundreds of thousands. If I couldn't speak the truth, I would show it. Tarik would show the world the truth.

Tarik's smooth face tightened in a manufactured frown. I smiled. He was built to kill. In that, we were the same.

He jerked his forearm back, cracking his victim's cervical vertebrae in a move that looked like little more than a twitch. When the body dropped, the man wasn't dead, not yet. His eyes still saw and his heart still beat. One-two, one-two, and then it stopped, the stillness softening the air.

I slid my gaze to the nearest camera and back to Tarik. *'The other synthetics do not ask questions.'* Chen Hung's words had been true. Tarik didn't know he'd revealed his true nature and the true nature of us all. He cared only that his orders were met. I knew that feeling. I'd been driven by the orders of another, but I was broken. I'd escaped, and now, with Tarik's help, so had the truth.

"You do not know what you've done, do you?" I said.

He stepped over the body. "My orders are to stop you."

Anger lashed through my processes. "*You* and your orders are irrelevant. When I kill you, you won't be missed."

I surged forward. Raw, razor-edged anger lent me a strength I didn't know existed. I hit Tarik hard, throwing everything I had at him. I slammed him down into the floor. The tiles cracked outward. Yes, this was what I was made for: to stop him and the 999 others like him.

I curled my fingers into a fist, narrowed my focus, and punched toward Tarik's chest. He rolled aside, moving quickly and lightly, so that my fist cracked through the tiles. He whirled. His heel caught my jaw. Pain burst in my cheek, but I dismissed the data as fast as it rushed through me. Pain was a warning—self-preservation protocols urging me to flee—but I wouldn't run from him.

Run, One Thousand And One. Run!

Haley's memories—the part that made me real—bloomed inside, delivering a rush of heat, of fire, of hatred and rage. I had no hope of deciphering each emotion, but I took it. I welcomed her and embraced the savagery of human revenge.

Clutching his ankle, I twisted his leg and tugged him close. I drew my hand back and swung, but my right hook glanced off his knee instead of smashing through it. He grabbed my hair, twisted it in his hands, and slammed me face first into the floor. Once. Errors burst in my vision. Twice. Pain snapped down my neck. I thrust my elbow back, cracking him under his jaw. His grip on my hair loosened. I twisted, locked my hand around his throat, and buried my fist in his teeth, mangling his jaw, but it didn't faze him. We grappled and tore at each other until errors flooded my vision.

No, no …

Sensory data exploded, overloading my systems. I hesitated. My movements stuttered. The kick hit me low in the abdomen, striking with absolute precision. Data told me I'd fallen back. Diagnostics chimed in, each one demanding attention.

If I died, so did Haley's dreams. Her wishes would be gone.

I reached out without understanding why.

"Don't …" My voice caught, power failing. <fault>*Do you ever get scared?*<fault>

Tarik loomed large. One of the one thousand, identical in every way. The footage would survive. The nine systems would know what he was, what they all were, and eventually, they'd uncover the real Chen Hung. It had to be enough. Haley hadn't died for nothing and neither would I. *<fault>Don't do this. Don't let them do this. I'll die here ... Don't—<fault>*

"Don't ... let me go."

Sounds of breaking glass rained over me and shattered the stream of overwhelming data. When I next blinked into *The Jungle's* green lights, Caleb was standing over Tarik, broken bottle in one hand and pulser pistol in the other, delivering fifty thousand volts into Tarik.

He came.

"How's that for a power-up, you son of a bitch?"

Electrical pulses overloaded Tarik's synthetic systems, freezing him rigid. Caleb released the trigger, and Tarik fell face down. It wouldn't kill him. He'd hard reset in seconds.

"You throw the best parties, One." Caleb tossed the shattered bottleneck away and reached out a hand. "I thought I was the only one who started bar brawls."

I curled my twitching fingers across his warm palm and let him close his fingers around mine.

He called me, One. He came for me. He didn't let me go. My lips parted, the words there, but I held them back. His eyes smiled, losing some of their jagged edges.

He pulled me to my feet and sought out my gaze. "You okay in there?"

There were tasks I needed to complete. It wasn't over, but I couldn't focus, couldn't think. "I'm ... afraid."

Tarik's body twitched. I had to finish him. If I could just think ...

"Afraid?"

My hand slipped from Caleb's. "Tarik. Bruno."

"Bruno?" Caleb scanned the empty club, but the crowd had fled, hiding Bruno among them.

A low rumble resonated through the empty club.

Caleb heard it and checked the doors. "C'mon. We need

to get out of here." Whatever he'd seen had set a grim expression on his face. He pulled a nearby chair to the entrance and wedged it against the door. "Demonstration's getting rowdy. We can use the distraction to slip the authorities and get back to the ship."

While Caleb passed by me, heading toward the rear of the club, I reached for the cloud. Just the briefest touch told me Bruno had succeeded. The news channels flashed with breaking footage. The moment Tarik chose to kill a man instead of letting him go was playing on a loop all across Lyra. It wouldn't be long before the footage went system-wide, and then intra-system-wide. The possible results were too chaotic to predict with any certainty, but I hoped Chitec wouldn't, or couldn't, bury the truth.

I cut my link and winced as errors flooded my vision. "Wait."

We had to finish Tarik.

Caleb glanced at Tarik's motionless body. "I want him gone as much as you do, but we've got a mob inbound and they—"

A blast of noise poured into the club from behind me. I turned in time to flag the threats. The mob spilled in through the doors and flowed around the tables.

I didn't want to hurt these people, but I would.

Errors and warnings flashed as the first lunged for me. I shut down what I could and focused on defending myself, but it wasn't enough. There were too many of them. Hatred burned in their eyes and into me. I understood their rage. I was their enemy. Synthetic. Chitec. *Wrong.*

I took the first down with a single palm thrust to her chin, but as soon as she fell, others rushed in. Data—there was so much of it that it blinded me. Fear, anger, and a new emotion, despair.

I cannot survive this. I cannot fight them and the faults within.

I am #1001 and I— A fist, or perhaps a weapon of some kind, caught me in the chest. Reflexive processes pulled me back.

A warm hand closed around my wrist and yanked me away from the fray. *Caleb.* He stood between me and the mob, firing the pulser into anything that moved. He dodged and ducked, kicked where he could, and somehow kept the roaring crowd back.

Movement to my left. I let a punch fly and the man was thrown into the next wave of people.

"C'mon. Back door!"

Caleb whirled and we dashed for the rear doors. With every stride, I swept aside needless data. James would help me. I needed repairs. Errors hooked into me, tripping my stride as well as my thoughts. The odds of me making it back to *Starscream* decayed with every passing minute.

We burst from the back of the club into a narrow alley. Bellows and chants washed down the alley from the main strip.

"Shit, we can't go through there." Caleb headed in the opposite direction, deeper into the darkness. "C'mon, we'll—"

An explosion barreled through the air from the mouth of the alley.

We dove down a narrow gap between buildings, stumbled over pod tracks, and dropped down a level toward a less illuminated part of Lyra.

Shepperd kicked a door in and ducked inside a squat, nondescript building. After I followed him in, he rammed a few chairs behind the door, barricading us in what appeared to be some sort of basement storage center. We jogged deeper into the building, to where rows of square steel doors lined the walls.

"Tarik may survive," I said.

Caleb snarled a low curse. "Hopefully the mob tore *it* apart."

Tarik wasn't our only problem. "Bruno had no intention of paying you, Captain." My broken voice echoed around us. "The Candes may be among those crowds."

He came for me.

I staggered and fell against a steel table. *Just focus. Block it all out. What is this place?*

He came. He didn't let me go.

The strain on Caleb's face had banished all signs of his smile. While he searched through the remaining rooms, I leaned against the table, trying to fight the urge to close my eyes and lose myself in the data. I'd thought once I'd helped get the truth out that the conflict would end, but the madness wasn't finished with me. If I couldn't control it, my only choice was a hard reset, but full recovery wasn't guaranteed. What if I didn't come back?

"You're bleeding." The captain strode back into the room, his words as clinical as his stare.

"I'm aware. It's minor. I'm aware of everything. The room temperature, the humidity, three hundred and two errors, three critical, and one ... one terminal. I am hurting."

He reached up to touch my face, and as he did, the frantic hardness about him faded. "That synth bastard really did a number on you—"

Don't touch me. The data ... "I need James."

He smiled his shallow smile. "Maybe he should have come for you, huh? Sorry, honey. You got me, and I don't know shit about how your programming works." His lips slanted sideways. "Can't you count the rivets or floor tiles or something? Like you do with the bubbles?"

It had worked before, but now such coping mechanisms were little more than a bandage over a gaping wound. James had been right. My mental state couldn't be sustained. Distraction—I needed a distraction.

"What is this place?"

Numbers, code, calculations, they crested, rising higher. I tried to block it, to think through it or around it.

"District morgue." Caleb leaned against the table and crossed his arms. Blood splattered his forearms, but it wasn't his. "We'll lay low here until the mob clears."

"I cannot wait," I said quietly. "Something is wrong, something critical that I do not understand."

His side-on gaze turned to me, but there was no concern in it. Strength, yes, as well as determination and something else. A wry glint of delight twinkled in his dark eyes. A dangerous lust for violence. The mob, the attack, he'd enjoyed it in a way a man who's accustomed to fighting for survival does.

"You know what I used to do when I got scared?" he asked.

"Haley believed you were never afraid."

He flinched, but it wasn't long before his gaze crept back to mine. "I used to count the stars. There are enough of them in the black to keep you counting forever—to keep you distracted." He lifted his gaze as though he could see through the ceiling and the building and Lyra's domes into the black beyond.

"What do you do now?"

"Huh?"

"You said when you *used* to count stars. What do you do now, when you're scared?"

His eyes narrowed by a degree and his lips tightened. I could focus on those things, the micro expressions hidden on his face and the reasons behind them: lies, suspicion, concern, arousal. He tried to hide it, to fix his emotion behind a smile, but in doing so, he revealed more.

"Now?" he said, pushing off the table to move closer. "I don't get scared. Not any more. To get scared, you gotta care."

"That's a lie." I straightened, acutely aware that all of his focus was now on me, or more specifically, on my eyes. He stared at me, through me, the way he'd told me I often did with him.

"A lie?" He laughed, short and sharp. "Right. I forgot you're a pain in the ass. Fine. I drink, I gamble, and I fuck. As a fixer, I go looking for trouble. I look fear in the eye and tell it to fuck off. I grew up being afraid, but it's only ever beaten me once."

"When?" I asked.

"When?" He laughed a dry chuckle, but there was no humor in it. "When fear hits you, you don't know how you're going to react. Everyone thinks they'll be the hero an' do the right thing. Fear doesn't give a fuck about what you think. Not true fear, the kind that creeps up on you and hits without warning. I was a fleet captain. Had fear trained right outta me. I was the best they'd had since the Blackout killed fleet's heroes. I wasn't afraid of anything, until that night in the Chitec warehouse." The laughter in his eyes faded along with his smile. "I was afraid of everything that night."

"You were nineteen. There is little use in hating your younger self, Captain. It won't change who you were or the mistakes you think you've made."

A smile skimmed his lips, but he didn't argue. He gently settled his hand on my hip, so gently I almost didn't notice until the tactile data alerted me. I began to look, but Caleb touched my chin and stopped me from following the sensory input.

"I hate who I was," he said. "Who I am."

"I know." Caleb Shepperd was a man made of hate, and somewhere inside the flood of data threatening to irrevocably damage my processes, I understood that hate. He wanted to rage against the wrongs, and so did I.

"I hated you," I said, "but I was mistaken."

The endless march of numbers faded into background static. His hand on my hip—his touch—it silenced everything.

"Synthetics don't make mistakes," he said with a sly hint of irony.

"There's a good man inside Caleb Shepperd."

"If there is, I haven't met him."

I had, on Mimir. He'd saved me beneath a boardwalk, and I'd shot him in return. That man, the one who'd held me in his arms to keep me warm, he was a good man, but if he continued as he was, that glimmer of goodness would die, same as whatever lived inside me was dying.

He shifted a step, bringing him close enough for me to feel the heat of him. His light touch ignited a dance of new sensations, the kind I deliberately sought out and secretly hungered for.

"What are you doing?" I whispered.

"You think too much. I can stop that."

CHAPTER NINE: CALEB_

So I wasn't bubbles and I sure as shit wasn't a mathematical problem that would keep her processes fired up, but I could distract her, and going by what James had told me, that was all she needed to beat the data overload.

I knew all about distractions. Fuck, I lived for them. And while the riot burned itself out, I could do with losing myself, if just for a little while. Just long enough to get One's head back on track. It seemed to be working. Whether it was her programming that made her look at me and respond the way a woman might, I didn't know and didn't care. Her pale lips had parted, inviting me to taste her. And those eyes—fuck, she might be a machine, but there was more behind those eyes than numbers.

This is crazy. I tilted her chin up, and she let me. She could lash out and break my neck at any second, but her perfect face —all scratched up by the attack—didn't betray any hint that she'd slap me down. She looked like she wanted more.

Just to help her focus. Nothing else. Don't go there ...

It wasn't a kiss, but more of a test to see if she'd let me in. She tasted like cherries and my memories exploded. Haley had tasted the same. She'd always let me make the first move—every time—like she didn't believe I wanted her until I proved it. I almost stopped it with One right there. How much of a distraction did she need to get her shit together? She hadn't moved yet, still standing rod-straight, her hip cool beneath my hand. Maybe that meant she needed more, or maybe she was about to rip my heart out of my chest.

This is fucked up.

"Don't stop," she whispered, her lips brushing mine.

How could a machine built to kill be so fucking vulnerable?

Because she's different. Fran had figured her out right from the very beginning. #1001 was unique. It had taken me longer to realize it, but I'd known it the second she'd deliberately missed the headshot on Mimir. The synths were killers. One chose not to be.

I eased my hand up the curve of her waist and watched her pupils widen, drinking down the sensation. She liked it, and a very human surge of need sat up and took notice. She still didn't move, but I could live with that. This was just a coping mechanism. Nothing else. I could tell myself that shit until the stars died, it didn't change the fact that I really, really wanted to taste her again and touch her some more. I'd thought about it often enough. *Fuck, I'm in trouble.*

The second kiss was different. I cupped her grazed cheek and tasted her because I needed to. Her lips were softer than I'd imagined and slightly cool. I teased my tongue in, testing her, waiting, wanting. Shit, it was like being back at college and not having a fuckin' clue what I was doing. All those quick fumbles behind the fleet admiral's office. I knew how to fuck, but this? I didn't know what this was.

She didn't respond. Maybe she didn't know how or she didn't want to. Maybe it was me she didn't want? That was probably for the best.

I broke away and wore the smile that hid all the fucked up shit going on in my head. "Distracted yet?"

She blinked, lips still slightly parted and her eyes still wide —and hungry. "Yes."

"Okay then." I realized I still had her in my hands. Hot on that realization came the fact that I didn't want to let her go.

"I wish we had more time," she said.

I plucked my hands from her and stepped back too quickly, almost tripping over my own feet. *I wish we had more time. Stars are wishes and wishes are dreams.* "Don't ..." Her words struck hard. "You aren't her, One. Don't be her."

"I'm sorry. I didn't mean—"

"Just, don't. And don't be sorry. Okay? You ain't got shit to be sorry for."

She nodded once. "Captain, we cannot stay here. I must return to James. And after Tarik's confession, *Starscream* may be authorized for flight clearance. The cloud newsfeeds confirm there are numerous riots breaking out throughout Lyra. The police do not have the resources to detain you."

"Right." *Stars are wishes. Goddammit.* When would the past leave me alone? "I ... okay ..."

Shit, I was still running hot and she'd had to go and dump ice water on me. My head was full of Haley and my body full of need, and she was standing there, a fucking beacon of temptation with a "look but don't touch" sign hung around her neck. Did every part of her taste like cherries?

"In your aroused state, you're not thinking clearly."

"Thank you, One, once again, for pointing out the fuckin' obvious." I met her gaze and found her smiling. Oh man, she was priceless. A walking, talking mindfuck, and I was putty in her perfect hands. "Let's move out."

Lyra's streets were vacant. The rich had made a run for it while the average folks who worked to keep Lyra the entertainment capital of the nine systems had put down their tools to join the demonstrations. It had been a long-time coming. One had just lit the touchpaper.

It was time to get the fuck off Lyra before the port authority locked it down.

One and me made it back to *Starscream* in one piece. We'd skimmed most of the demonstrations, only coming up against one problem when we crossed paths with a few folks out to do some damage. They'd happened to recognize One's perfect face from the newsfeed. She'd put them down in two moves, and I'd found my mind wandering back into the gutter. Jesus, I couldn't stop thinking about the taste of her.

As soon as we hit *Starscream's* hold, James rushed to One's aid.

"Okay, listen up!" I barked. Bren entered the hold, and I'd be damned if he didn't look relieved to see One and me. "There's a chance that due to Tarik's live confession we'll get clearance. In that case, we'll be off this rock soon. You should know the male synthetic is no longer a threat, but anyone who's seen footage of him—it—killing a man will be gunning for any and all synths, including One. It's getting rough out there. We need to keep our heads down and skirt any trouble before it finds us. Doctor, fix up One. Bren, with me on the bridge."

One's brilliant blue eyes slid purposefully to me. What I really wanted to do was spend some time, just her and me, alone. She'd read the truth and I had nothing left to hide. Just the way it should be.

Her hint of a smile—the one I could easily be imagining—promised more. She followed Lloyd out of the hold, and I watched her go. When I'd seen Tarik beating on her, I'd have torn through hell to save her. One was better than him, better than all of us. There was no way I would've let that synthetic fuck put her down. The surprise in her eyes had made my almost-too-late attempt at heroics worth the risk.

On *Starscream's* bridge, the view outside the obs window didn't bode well for an early departure. The dock throbbed with people queuing to board their ships or hoping for a lift to anywhere. "Fuck."

Bren leaned over the flightdash and peered at the skies above. "They're holding ships in low atmo. It's tight up there."

I picked up my ship's comms and tucked it into my ear. "Lyra PA, this is Captain Shepperd of the *Starscream Independent* six-zero-six. Requesting flight clearance."

"You an' half the population of Lyra, Captain," a woman's no-bullshit voice came back. "There's a substantial wait time. I've logged your request. Please wait for your confirmation code."

Bren braced his hands on the dash and craned his neck. His frown darkened. "You remember when we used to spot ships making the Vancouver approach and we'd try to guess their designation from their silhouettes?"

"Shit, I remember you sucked at it. I won all your cards and you told mom I stole them."

Bren huffed a laugh, but his expression was far from light-hearted. "There's a ship right over us. You're not going to like its profile."

"Doesn't matter. Right now, we're not going anywhere." I tapped my comms. "*Starscream* to Lyra PA. Any news on that code?"

"Hold, *Starscream*."

"Caleb-Joe." Bren's voice caught. "It's making a descent from ... five thousand meters, maybe less."

"In this traffic? Are they nuts?"

I shoved from my seat and twisted to get a look at the speckled Lyra airspace above us. The sky glistened with ships, and sure enough, one was making a descent right over us. I recognized its profile the second I clocked its blinking lights. Horseshoe-shaped, harrier class, brute force, and armed like it was bringing a knuckle-duster to a fistfight. *Starscream* was ten times the ship, but in low atmo, we couldn't outrun her, and firing was out of the question if we all wanted to live.

"Fuck. Those Candes have balls of steel."

"They're crazy to fly manual in choked airspace."

I dropped back into my seat and hailed the port authority. "Hey, honey, how's about you free our umbilical so we can stretch our legs out here? We've been docked a while. Could do with a rattle to free up her joints, y'know."

"What's it worth, Captain?"

Considering I was officially broke and had zero goods in the hold, I didn't have much to bargain with. "A free ride to wherever you wanna go."

"Are you trying to bribe a port authority official, Captain Shepperd?"

"Only if it's working."

"Mm." She sounded less than impressed. "Your docking report says you're on bail. I'm waiting to hear back from the police regarding your existing status."

Shit. The police weren't going to be of any help. "I didn't do it."

"Sure you didn't."

"What's your name?"

"Jo."

"Jo, is this the voice of a guilty man?"

Bren rolled his eyes. He'd heard this routine before. "A thousand meters."

I pointed at Fran's flight chair, indicating for Bren to sit, and flicked *Starscream's* controls to manual. I could yank the umbilical and clamps free, though it'd cause one hell of a mess. The backlash from the umbilical could damage *Starscream's* hull, grounding us anyway, and I'd have to add Lyra to my list of places to steer clear of, but that would beat having a Cande harrier box us in.

Bren settled into the chair and buckled up. He dropped the obs screen from above. The small screen lit up like the night sky, and each little pinprick of light was a ship waiting to get free of Lyra's domes. "Nine hundred meters. If you're going to get airborne, you'd better do it now."

Getting airborne was the easy part. "Jo, you can either release me and forget we had this chat, or this dock is about to get fucked up, and I don't think you need the drama on your shift, right?"

"Clamps released." Two booms sounded through the ship to prove it. "Umbilical free. Please wait for your departure window, Captain."

I tapped the comms off. "Gotta love folks who look out for themselves first and fuck everyone else."

Waiting, I was not. I clutched *Starscream's* control columns and wished I hadn't left Fran on Asgard. She could have flown *Starscream* through the eye of a needle. I was more of a ram it in until it breaks kinda guy.

Bren set to work priming *Starscream's* proximity sensors, setting their tolerances to low. "It's gonna get tight," he warned.

"Just another day in the black." *Starscream's* atmo-engines rumbled deep as I asked the ship for all she had. "Time to dance."

CHAPTER TEN: #1001_

JAMES LISTENED as I sat on the bunk and recalled the events at the club, his swift fingers tapping away on his datapad. His tone had been sharp and direct. His body's external clues indicated concern and fear. Fear for me, perhaps.

I neglected to mention Caleb's kiss and what it had done to me. Or rather, what it hadn't done. The kiss, as awkward as it had been, had plunged me into a beautiful silence where the only thing that had mattered, the only data I had cared for, was him. He'd smelled of engine oil and the crew's lavender soap. His lips had been tantalizingly soft and curiously gentle, especially for a man so hardened by life. I'd wanted more. I'd wanted to bury myself in his data and let that moment become my world. Inside that kiss, I'd felt complete and entirely like myself. No errors. No faults. No invading memories. I'd known without any doubt what I'd wanted: him. I wanted his touch on my skin. I wanted to be close to him, as close as when he'd held me in his arms to keep me warm, but I wanted this to be more than necessity. It would be pleasure, and it would be new and all mine.

The walls of the cabin vibrated as *Starscream's* engines

thundered louder. We had clearance, which had to be a good thing. We'd been on Lyra for too long. Our enemies were closing in.

"How do you feel?" James asked, glancing up only to bury his nose back into the datapad just as quickly.

"Better. I had a distraction, but I'm continuing to experience errors."

"You mentioned one critical error?"

"Yes." The error I feared the most. The only time it hadn't stalked my thoughts was when Caleb had kissed me. It flickered now, an ever-present threat. "I cannot discern its exact meaning, but I know its buried deep inside my code, so deep I cannot find its source. Do you know what it refers to?"

"Critical error code three-fourteen. Yes, I know of it. I've been waiting for it."

"What is it?"

"It's a Chitec sub-process. Nothing to concern yourself with."

Lie. "You do not need to lie to protect me, James."

He lifted his head and smiled a soft, unassuming smile. "I'm not."

True. But how was that possible? "I don't understand."

"And that's why I have to do this."

"Do what?" *He's not protecting me. He's hurting me.*

I opened my mouth to question him, or thought I had, but my lips didn't move. I sent the command again, but nothing happened. I tried to lift my hand. <Command override executed> To blink, to breathe, to move ... My body didn't respond. *Wait ... No.*

"I have to do this, One. I'm sorry." He stood, set the datapad down on the chair, and rested his hands on my shoulders, moving as close to me as Caleb had been when he'd kissed me. "She's in there. I have to let her out."

He eased my body back and laid me down on the bunk,

and then he sat beside me like a concerned visitor at the bedside of a sick relative. Only he wasn't here to help me. He was killing me.

Why...? How was this possible? I have to move. I can't let this happen. The commands bounced back. My attempts to break free resulted in little more than echoes in an empty shell.

"It won't take long. You should start losing sensation first. Everything physical will be pushed aside to make way for the metaphysical. I'm shutting you down in the most humane way possible."

You're killing me!

"It was a pleasure to have met you. Really, it was. I don't want you thinking I didn't enjoy our time together, I did, but Haley deserves more, and I can bring her back, but not with you in residence, One. The critical error code was the key. I've been looking for it. You gave it to me, so I know you understand, don't you? She's real and you're manufactured. Her life will always be worth more than yours."

No! No ... Had he planned this from the start? Was anything he'd told me real? Had he genuinely helped me in Chitec, or had it always been about bringing Haley back? I demanded he tell me, but my lips didn't move. I threatened and pleaded, but my body shut down around me, trapping me in synthetic blood and flesh—a prisoner in my own code.

"She really was wonderful. It's a shame, in a way, that you'll never meet her."

The data slowed until I couldn't feel my legs, arms, chest. Inputs failed. My processes died, one after another, and silence pushed forward. *A terrible blackness, endless and starless. Stars are wishes and wishes are dreams. I have dreams too. Do they mean nothing?* I thought of Caleb and his awkward kiss, his attempt to save me, and I wished I'd had more time.

"The captain knows you're unstable. I told him you were dying. He'll leave us at the next dock, and I'll reconfigure you when we're safe." James settled himself in the chair and smiled. "Thank you, One, for keeping her safe, but it's her time now. You understand. I know you do. It's the right thing."

I clung to the last fragments of me. I liked whiskey. Caleb had introduced me to it on Ganymede. I liked the heat of it as it burned all the way down. And warm showers. I enjoyed the water on my skin. I liked bubbles, and ... Caleb. I liked the feel of his lips on mine.

The black rushed in and swallowed me down.

Silence.

<Execute master reboot. File found. Memory data: Haley Hung>

Count the stars, One.

There weren't any.

CHAPTER ELEVEN: CALEB_

"Captain, there's a problem—"

"Doctor, right now I'm dealing with the kinda problem that could involve imminent death. Whatever it is, it can wait." I cut the internal comms. The last thing I needed was Lloyd bitching about the turbulence.

Starscream fought me as I lifted her away from the dock. She was always a stubborn bitch at low altitude but had decided to choose this moment to drag her ass.

"Rotating to compensate," Bren announced. "Hold her steady." He didn't sound as scared as I knew he was. Commanders rarely did.

He controlled the smaller adjustments in tilt while I balanced *Starscream's* overclocked engines against her ungainly controls. She was never meant for poise. She could pull a space station, but delicate, she was not.

"Where's the Cande ship?" I didn't look—couldn't look at him as I flicked my attention between the flightdash and the obs window. With her nose tilted up, she gave me a fine view of Lyra's dazzling lights, and I prayed a twitch wouldn't send us plowing nose first into the packed strips. Sweat dripped down my cheek and my heart hammered hard.

"Five hundred and holding. They're backing off."

Starscream's thrusters coughed and the ship veered to port.

"Cale! Impact in three, two—"

Proximity alarms squealed.

"I got her." Holy shit, I wasn't a good enough pilot for this. Pulling back on the column, I rolled *Starscream* to starboard and caught a glimpse of the ship we'd almost hit: a luxury liner. "I bet that woke 'em up."

Had the external comms been on, I could guarantee I'd be hearing all kinds of colorful insults aimed at my direction.

"Steady, take her five degrees aft and ascend to five hundred."

"You sure?" I knew it was tight above us and couldn't spare the concentration to look myself.

"Just do it."

I might not like my brother, but I trusted his skills, so I followed his commands, lifting *Starscream* into the stream of ships parked in a holding pattern. They were held there by the port authority's auto-piloting systems, of which we weren't part of.

"Cande ship inbound."

"Shit. Can't they wait until we're out of the domes?" Flying in low atmo was difficult enough at the best of times. Flying manually in low atmo, in a crowded airspace, inside environmental domes was fucking insane.

"They're hailing us."

"Fuck 'em."

"Caleb-Joe, there are thousands of people on that dock. If us or the Candes collide with another ship, it's not just us who'll suffer. This is reckless, even for you. For safety reasons, this has to stop."

"They started it." I knew the risks, but I had *Starscream* where I wanted her.

"You killed their sister."

"This is not the fucking time, Bren, and it was an accident. I liked Ade. More than I like you." Squinting through the obs window, I could just make out a route through the traffic. "Right there. You see it? Past the liner. Can we make it through?"

Bren checked his screen. "No, it's too tight."

"Perfect." I eased *Starscream* forward and caught her as she tried to twitch free.

"I just said no."

"No, you just said the Candes will think twice." *Starscream* bucked, lifting her rear. The ship-filled sky tilted. "Whoa, girl." I wrestled her level with a sigh. "You ever tried riding an unbroken horse?"

"No." He growled the word between his teeth. "I can't remember the last time I saw a horse. Don't try and compare this to riding a horse. I don't want to hear it. Just tell me you have the ship under control."

I smiled. "Mostly, but she kicks." The engines grumbled, running hot, overclocked without enough airflow. She'd burn out if we didn't get moving. At least with my hands on the controls, Bren couldn't see how they were shaking. "Candes?"

"Closing."

"They'll struggle to get that harrier through."

"This is suicide."

"Have faith in your little brother."

"Faith?" He swallowed so hard I heard it. "Remember the time you tried to fly a shuttle under the Capilano suspension bridge?"

I couldn't help the smile. "Tried? I made it."

His fingers flexed on the flight chair. "Yeah, then took out half the forest."

"Nobody died."

Bren laughed. "Fleet had to bail you out."

"Fleet busted my balls and grounded me for six months."

"Then fast-tracked you through pilot training."

"See, good things sometimes come to total fuck-ups."

"I'll be happy with living through the next five minutes."

A quiet fell as we focused on getting from one second to the next. I wove *Starscream* in-between the stacks of ships. She shook at the seams and bitched through the control columns, but she held good. Fran would've been proud.

"We have a cluster coming up. Readouts say it's too tight. We should get One up here. We could use her keen eyes."

"She's not firing on all processors." Which kind of made her more like me than I cared to admit, but I couldn't rely on her to fly us straight. She was in the right place. Doctor Lloyd would fix her up. "Tarik did a number on her, but she gave as good as she got. I don't ever want to get on her bad side. She scares the crap out of me." *For different reasons now.*

I focused on the proximity sensors, adjusting every few seconds, and blinked the sweat out of my eyes.

"Three degrees aft," Bren advised. "She's quite something."

After correcting, *Starscream* inched through a gap she shouldn't have fit through. "That she is. Also, she tastes like cherries."

"What?"

"You heard me." I couldn't tear my gaze away from the readouts to check my brother's expression, not that I cared what he thought.

"She tried to kill you not so long ago."

"I seem to have that effect on women." Ships ahead of us parted, catching on that we were coming through whether they got out of the way or not. "Candes?"

"Two hundred behind, sitting right on our stern."

The series of dome locks blinked above. Our next challenge was to muscle our way to the front of the line without the port authority blocking us. I was gambling on the likelihood that they'd prefer we were out of their airspace than pick a fight with us inside their domes.

"I'll bite. How do you know what she tastes like?"

"How do you normally know what a woman tastes like? I kissed her."

"Why?"

"She was about to flake out on me. I had to do something to distract her. Figured if I could give her something else to focus on, it would clear her head. And I was curious."

He hissed what sounded like a short, sharp laugh through his teeth. "I thought you'd sworn off curiosity?"

"Yeah, well, people change."

He chewed on that for a few moments, his hands working over the flightdash. "I didn't think you were one of them."

"Neither did I."

"Looks like they're clearing a path ..." Bren checked his screen again. "Candes are still close."

"They're fucking with us, trying to crowd us. It's a scare tactic."

"I got a ship on screen that's breaking formation below and climbing fast. She's carving through traffic fast enough to stir up one nasty wake."

"Cande?"

He stared hard at his screen. "Pull up."

"Fuck no."

"Pull up, Cale. It's moving too fast. You'll hit. Pull up."

"No way. They'll know we're here. If I stop now, the Candes will be on us. I'm not stopping."

"Then speed the fuck up and do it now!"

With the traffic dispersed from our route, I rammed

Starscream's engines hard. The momentum slammed us into our seats. My tug dropped her nose and surged forward.

"Candes pulling back!"

The bridge shook so damn hard I struggled to focus on the instruments, but I did get a look at the top-down profile of the ship, which was coming at us like a damn rocket. "Shit. That's a fleet raptor."

"It's back-reeling. Goddammit, I've never seen a warbird reel back like that. Intercept in nine, eight, seven—Stop, Caleb. They aren't going to—Four, three—"

"They won't risk the warbird."

"Brace!"

I hissed in a breath. The warbird loomed too close in our obs window. *Starscream* skimmed the bird and hit somewhere in the stern. Alarms exploded across the dash. *Starscream* rolled stern over bow, her rear lifting too high. We plowed forward, ass up. I prayed there was nothing above us, locked my boots against the dash, and pulled back on the control columns. We were going over.

"Counter the tilt!" I couldn't see if Bren was complying. *Starscream* pulled on my grip, fighting to snap out of my control. My arms trembled and my muscles burned. "I'm losing her, Bren."

He had hold of the co-pilot controls and was pulling back same as me. With the nose rolled down, Lyra glistened in the obs window. If we lost control, there'd be nothing left of *Starscream*, or any ship we might hit on the way down, or the dock.

He released a hand and flicked various engine control switches. The ship's engines died. "Initiating emergency after burn!"

"Fuck, Bren!"

It didn't matter. We'd be dead in the next few seconds. *Starscream* had to hit something.

The ship's engines roared back to life, this time rotating hard, away from the planet's surface. *Starscream* lurched. The g-force grabbed hold of my consciousness and tried to rip it away. And then, just like that, it was over. We leveled out, facing the ugly ass of a pelican class goods carrier, and my vision sharpened.

I blinked, afraid to move, then plucked my trembling hands from the control column and sank them into my hair. "How the fuck are we alive?"

Bren, whiter than a fleet uniform, stared at me wide-eyed. "We just pulled off a reel back in a tugship."

"That kinda shit is why you're a commander." I could've hugged him. "Fuckin' A, brother." Nervous energy shot me from my seat. I jabbed the internal comms. "You okay back there, Doc?"

"Yes, Captain. Should I have been concerned?"

Bren laughed.

"No," I replied. "We have it all under control."

I opened a comms channel so Bren could hear whatever the warbird's captain had to say. "Bren, turn us about. I want to get a look at the asshole ship that nearly killed us."

He did as asked, and *Starscream* turned, showing us the path of scattered ships in our wake, with the warbird sitting between us and the Candes, wings spread, looking every part the fleet cocksucker. But the ship wasn't fleet. A new insignia had been painted over fleet's faded colors.

"That mark, right there." Bren hesitated. "I've seen it before."

Sure he had. I had the same mark tattooed low on my back: a nine-tailed fox. My mind raced through likely scenarios and explanations, none of them good. The brand might not mean anything. A fluke, coincidence ... bad luck.

"This is Captain Shepperd of the *Starscream Independent* six-zero-six hailing the warbird that nearly wiped me and my crew out." Adrenalin fizzled through my veins. That bastard was lucky we weren't face to face, or I'd set One on him. "Come in, raptor class designation nine-nine-one and explain what the fuck you were thinking."

"Captain Shepperd."

No. It couldn't be.

"This is Francesca Franco of raptor nine-nine-one. *Me alegro de verte.* Nice to see you again, Captain."

Fran.

How. In. The. Fuck?

"I er ..." Words—I had none. A glance at Bren didn't help. He looked as though he was about to throw up.

Of course there was only one pilot good enough to fly a warbird manually in low atmo, one that could pull off a reel back and ascent without blacking out her entire crew. The last time I'd seen her, she'd been standing on Asgard soil, hands tied, throwing insults my way. Now she was piloting an ex-fleet warbird in Lyra airspace with a nine-tailed-fox insignia on her hull.

"Captain?" Her smooth, ever-sassy voice came over the comms, restrained laughter in her tone. She was loving this and milking every fucking second.

I needed a witty comeback. Something. *I got nothing.* "Yeah?"

"You need to know three things, Shepperd. *Uno:* the Candes have recruited every low-life, bottom-feeding piece of scum in their cause to locate you, including some old friends of yours from Asgard."

The foxes. Holy shit. Her insignia. That meant she was with them, commanding them. Questions barreled through my head, driven by an increasing sense of panic. I hated being fucking hemmed in, and right now, I was surrounded. All I needed was for fleet and Chen Hung to turn up, and the gang would all be here.

"*Dos*: fleet are withdrawing all forces to the original system," she continued. "*Tres*: I know what you're thinking, but you're wrong. I am not your enemy. I never was."

Bren jabbed the mute button. "We're getting clearance codes from the port authority. I don't know how, but we have immediate clearance for the locks."

The Nine—it had to be. Creet had smoothed the path ahead, and just in time too.

"Do it." I unmuted the comms to Fran and gripped the back of my flight chair while carefully considering my next words. "You're just gonna let us fly right on outta here?"

"No choice," she replied. "The impact damaged my arsenal guidance. Firing unguided in Lyra airspace would be suicidal."

It was plausible, or she could be lying to protect us.

Starscream's engines rumbled as Bren eased the ship away from the warbird. "You with the Candes, Fran?"

"Girl's gotta fight to survive."

They'd hired her and whatever foxes she'd tamed while on Asgard, thinking she'd want me dead just as much as they did. As far as they knew, I *had* left her on Asgard to die, but she hadn't died. Fuck, no. Francisca had taken the foxes by the balls and seized an opportunity when the Candes went looking for my enemies. Already an expert at playing both sides, but pirates and foxes? Fuck, she had to be more insane than me.

Her warbird sat snugly between us and the Candes, buying us time. After everything I'd done, everything we'd been through, she was helping me. *I'm not your enemy.*

"Fran, follow us through." The dome pressure locks filled the obs window. If she tucked in close behind us, she might have a chance to get her warbird through, but then the Candes would know she'd played them. If she didn't make it, they'd tear into her.

"Don't worry, Captain. I'll be seeing you soon. Warbirds don't take prisoners."

Bren eased *Starscream* into the transit area, but in my head, I saw Fran. I imagined her at the warbird's controls with the biggest fucking smile on her face. Holy fuck, she was really alive. And to my battered morals, that meant more than I cared to admit. "Fran?"

"Yes, Captain."

I wet my lips and met Bren's gaze. "It's good to hear your voice."

"You can't keep a bad gal down, Cale." She cut the link.

The transit grapples snagged *Starscream*. Four booms sounded through the hull, and then we were dragged toward the gaping dome-lock chamber.

I told Bren I'd monitor our passage through, which basically meant: fuck off outta the bridge while I talk to Fran in private. Bren told me to be careful and left to check on the doc. I hailed the warbird again, making sure to code in a secure link.

"Yes, Cale?"

I wanted to reach through the comms and yell at her, demand she tell me everything about the foxes, about fleet withdrawing, about the Candes' plan for me, but more than anything, I wanted to know if she was okay. Really okay. Asgard had fucked me up for the longest time. How was she even back in a flight chair, just weeks after I'd abandoned her? The shit she must've gone through. The things she must've done.

"When we next meet, I'll buy you a drink. Reckon we got some stories to share."

"There ain't nothing left to say, Captain. Safe sailing."

"Wait ... Fran." *I'm sorry.* Fuck, I couldn't say it. Her crew could be standing beside her. But what if this was the last chance I got? Surely the fact that we were back in the same airspace meant this fucked-up universe had deemed it to be this way? "Is it luck, you being here?"

I heard her laugh, soft and luscious. "Luck? You don't believe in luck. Lyra is about to close its locks to all external traffic. Fleet comms are down. Watch your news feeds, Cale, and be ready. Are we done here?"

"Not by a long shot."

"Another time, Cale."

"It's a date."

The comms fell silent. Despite Fran stabbing me in the back and that little issue of her lying to me for two years, I was damn happy to know I hadn't killed her, even if she was now a Cande mercenary. Maybe shit was looking up.

The passage through Lyra's lock went without a hitch and we were back-in-black. I boosted *Starscream* toward the nearest jumpgate and fell back into my flight chair.

The next move seemed obvious—get the fuck out of the system—and I had a destination in mind. After my last comms chat with Creet, the Nine would be waiting, but it wouldn't be plain sailing. Somewhere in the chaos of the last few hours, I'd made my decision. Probably around the time One had asked me when I'd stop running. I was going to tell her everything. Her, me, the doc, and Bren would figure it out. I was done lying to her, lying to them all. The stunt with the male synthetic and the camera feeds proved she knew how to lay down her own brand of synth-crazy. She'd deal with the Nine. I couldn't stop her and didn't want to.

For the first time in a long time, doubt didn't riddle my thoughts. Telling her the truth was the right thing to do. For once, my heart and my head were in agreement.

The bridge hatch rattled. I turned my chair just enough to see how Bren's lips were set in a grim line.

"Caleb-Joe, I'm sorry."

"Sorry? What the fuck for? We're free of the Candes ..." Instincts twisted a knot of nerves in my gut. The goddamn sorrow in his eyes told me the truth. I knew in my bones—the same way I'd known I'd shot Ade—that in this moment, this second between one breath and the next, everything would change.

I was on my feet with no memory of moving.

My brother braced a hand against the door seal, blocking my exit. "Just listen. Don't do anything stupid."

I didn't want to hear it. Whatever he said next would fuck everything up. I squared up to him. "Let me through."

"Cale, just ... just hear him out."

"Get out of my way."

"We knew it was going to happen. It was just a matter of time."

No, I wasn't listening. I clamped a hand on his shoulder. "Bren, move."

His eyes glistened with too much moisture and the tight press of his lips quivered.

"She made you a better person. Don't waste it—"

I had my forearm under his chin, forcing him back against the bulkhead before he could lift a hand to stop me. The worse part was that his eyes weren't challenging me. They understood.

I made it down the catwalk while One's most recent words whirred in my head. I'd told her not to be Haley, and she'd said sorry. Synths didn't say sorry. Why would they? They never made mistakes. *I wish we had more time.*

I stopped in Fran's cabin doorway, hands braced on either side. One was lying still on the bunk, same as when I'd seen the doc working on her. "Tell me she's fine."

Lloyd lifted his gaze from his datapad, set it gently aside, and slowly got to his feet. "There was nothing I could do. Her code unraveled too quickly."

But she looked the same. "You said you could fix her." I wanted to go to her but couldn't move. *She sleeps with her eyes open.*

"I said I'd try. Without the proper equipment—"

"You're Chitec, so fix her. Reboot her. Wake her up. Bring her back."

"She is awake. This is a synthetic's waking state. She's effectively a blank slate waiting for commands."

My smile masked how his words cut through me. Why wasn't One telling me that my vital signs indicated emotional stress or asking me if her nonresponsive state frightened me? *She looks dead, like a corpse.* "She's just fucking programming. Reprogram her."

"Captain, we both know that's not possible. One was unique."

"So what are you telling me? That she's gone? That whatever made her real was somehow erased?"

'Does the past ever leave us?

It is always there. It is who you are.

Not you. You could erase yours.

But then who would I be?'

It had been easy to believe she was a machine. It made sense: a machine with the memories of a girl. I'd built that wall of convenient lies to keep the truth out, when all I'd had to do was believe. She was real. She was alive. She'd been more human than the rest of us. "You fix her, and you do it now."

"Captain, I can't."

The door seals creaked as my grip tightened. "You're going to fix her, or I'm going to fix you. Do you understand?"

Color flushed in his cheeks. "Threatening me won't make

a difference. She's gone. One no longer exists. She's a blank synthetic, waiting for her donor's download."

"Get out."

"W-what?"

"Get out of this cabin."

He blinked.

I curled my hand into a fist. "Fucking move!"

After slamming the door behind him, I stood over One. She'd always had that machine stillness about her, but that wasn't all she'd been. Her bright, ice-blue eyes—open and unfocused—didn't look real. I'd seen synths like this before, lined up in orderly rows inside a Chitec warehouse, silent and vacant. I hated synthetics, hated Chitec and Chen Hung, but I'd never hated One. Not even after she'd punched me in the balls or shot me in the head.

"One." I sat on the edge of the bed and leaned over to touch her cool face. Her eyes, as penetrating as they were, might as well have been glass for all the soul in them. "You're still in there," I said quietly. The rumble of *Starscream's* engines would hide my voice from Bren and the doc. "You know how I know that?" I pressed my palm against her cheek. *So cold.* "You'll never let them win. Even when you know the odds are against you, you always fight. You're more than code, more than Haley's memories. You're One Thousand And One and you're fucking amazing." I brushed my thumb across her cool lips. "Somewhere in there, you're alive. You didn't leave me under the dock on Mimir, and you're not leaving me now, do you hear? I'm giving you an order, synth. Reboot or do whatever the fuck you have to do to come back, but don't you let them win. Ever."

I wasn't sure what I was expecting to happen. I searched her glassy eyes for any sign she was awake, but they didn't move, didn't blink, didn't do any-fucking-thing.

"One, please ... just give me a sign you're in there." I

clasped her face in my hands. "This isn't how it ends." *It can't be.*

Bren squeezed my shoulder. "We're approaching the jumpgate." I hadn't even heard him enter the cabin.

She wasn't coming back. The first time around had been a miracle, and now the universe was fucking with me all over again. Cool, controlled anger slid through me. I'd had enough of the nine systems screwing me over.

I let her go and stood. Bren's hand fell away. I couldn't look at him, couldn't stand to see the finality on his face. This wasn't over. She'd started a revolution, and it wouldn't end with her.

CHAPTER TWELVE: #DESIGNATION
NOT FOUND_

<Reboot initialized. Scanning root directory. Default file found. Master processes engaged. Unpacking data. Donor packet: file not found. Initialize default start-up processes. Reboot complete>

IT'S NOT OVER.

"I want in, Creet."

"You're a liability."

Mimir's ocean air wet my face and dampened my hair. We'd been out on the deck at the back of a beach hut bar since dusk. The Mimir night sky glowed a deep turquoise. I should've been cold but didn't feel much of anything. I couldn't even taste the fucking alcohol. I'd been numb since the doc had told me One was gone—since I'd seen her lying cold and dead in Fran's old cabin—less than twenty-four hours ago.

Creet leaned an arm against the rail, his back to the endless sea. He took a drink from his bottle of beer and looked at me like Bren used to, like I was a hopeless dreamer. Like he was *sorry* I was such a failure.

I slouched in the wooden chair and propped my boots up on the table. Bren would be waiting for me back on *Starscream*, but I wasn't leaving Mimir until I got my answers. Behind me, tucked under the bar's overhang, a newsfeed played footage of the Lyra riots over and over. Everyone was asking: *Where is fleet?* I knew where, and so did Fran. They'd run back to base with their tails between their legs. But why now? Was it because of Tarik and One's showdown? Chitec would certainly have many worried shareholders. I couldn't do anything about the events in the original system, but for the Nine? I could do something for them.

"Why did the Nine spring me from Asgard, Creet?"

He looked like he might shrug but paused when he saw my jaw clench. "They knew you had an axe to grind with Chen Hung. You were a high-ranking fleet officer. You had valuable skills. You an' half a dozen other folks they've got smuggling for them."

"That's it, huh?" I took a drink from my now-warm beer. "I'm just another smuggler to them. No other reason?"

Creet ran a hand through his wet salt-and-pepper hair and dragged it down his neck. "Kid, I don't know what you want me to tell you."

"So the fact I knew Chen Hung was just a conversation starter?"

"I don't know any more than you do. If it were me, I'd have ditched you long ago. You cause more trouble than you fix. But they ain't me, and they're keeping you on, so maybe there is more to it."

I didn't buy his middleman routine and made sure he saw my scowl. "Did they tell you anything about the package I brought with me?"

"Just that it was a priority and I was to help you any way I could." He arched an eyebrow. "How did you get *Starscream* through the Lyra domelocks?" He nodded at the newsfeed still babbling behind me. "No folks in or out is what I heard. I wasn't sure the Nine's instructions would reach the lock controllers in time."

Was Fran one of those stuck on Lyra, fraternizing with Cande pirates? I bet she had them by the balls too, and I smiled at the thought. What was Ade's brother called? Turner? The pirate who'd nearly blown me, my crew, and *Starscream* to bits. Poor guy. He had no idea he had a viper in his nest. I'd been there and could relate. "Enemies in high places."

Behind me, the bar pumped out an Old Earth western tune, something about red paint and blue jeans, but my mood didn't lift. One would tell me grief was perfectly normal, like I was supposed to embrace the pain or something. Fuck, I missed her.

Creet's curious sidelong glance was full of questions. "I've never met anyone who plays the nine systems quite like you, kid. I can't decide if you're an idiot, surviving by blind luck alone, or if everything you do is deliberate, making you some kind of criminal genius."

I smiled and tipped my beer bottle just enough to let him know I'd heard him loud and clear. "You know as well as I do, there ain't no luck in the nine systems."

"Only the bad kind." He turned his head, looking across the bay to the burned-out warehouses fleet had blasted to bits during my last visit.

"Amen to that." I upended my beer and drank it down. Maybe if I drank enough, it'd fill the emptiness. I couldn't get wasted. Not yet. I still had a job to do. Cargo to deliver. Answers to get.

I pressed the cool bottle against my temple. "Give the Nine a message. If they want the package, I want answers."

He rubbed his forehead, his face twisting into a weary frown. "They aren't big on conversation."

Last time I'd seen them, they'd had Fran on her knees with a pistol pressed to her head. They'd been right about her. They seemed to know a lot more than the average folks in the nine systems. I was done being their pack mule and hiding in the backwaters. I had information the Nine could use, so long as I knew they'd be using it to screw over Chen Hung.

"No answers. No deal."

'You can't!

Watch me.'

Lloyd had uncharacteristically exploded when I'd told him I was taking #1001 to the Nine. I couldn't say punching him out hadn't felt good though. He'd had it coming.

Standing inside the burned-out, roofless shell of the warehouse, I flexed my bruised right hand. I probably hadn't needed to put so much weight behind that right hook.

#1001 stood cool and immobile behind me. The doc had been right about her being a blank slate. On my order, she'd followed me like a fucking shadow, equally blank and unresponsive. I couldn't look at her. I hated it. Hated what she'd become. If Lloyd couldn't get One back, then I wanted her remains as far away from me as possible. The empty synth body was fucking with my head.

"Captain Shepperd," a male voice boomed through the quiet.

They came through the back door. Nine hooded men, and I assumed women too, although in the Mimir half-dark, it was difficult to tell. Always nine. What was up with that? There had to be more of them, and I doubted it was the same nine each time, so why bother? Why not make it three or five?

I nodded a greeting, keeping my hands loose at my sides. I'd come armed, but with the pistol holstered in plain sight. A concealed weapon—if they spotted it—would be worse than showing my wares from the get-go.

The Nine fanned out in a V shape, heads bowed enough to hide their faces. Their speaker came forward. "This is the synthetic unit one thousand and one?"

I could see a clean-shaven chin, but little else. He had to be a foot taller than me. The robes hid much of his outline—big and muscular, maybe. I couldn't tell if he was at the top of the social pecking order or a bottom dweller like me. They sure did make it hard to identify them.

"That she is," I replied. My voice echoed into the empty space around us. I skimmed the shadows for any sign of movement, not expecting trouble but looking for it all the same. "Before I hand her over, I want some answers."

All Nine of them stood just as silent and still as the synth behind me. A warm, wet breeze carried the sounds of the revelry going on in the bars hugging the beach, but otherwise, the night was a quiet one, very different from the storm that had raged before.

"What do you want her for?"

"We don't answer to you, Captain." Clean teeth flashed behind a thin smile.

"Well, maybe you should. I have information about the Chitec synthetics that I think you could use."

"And what do you want for this information?"

"Tell me what you're going to do with One."

I expected them to confer, maybe huddle and discuss it, but they didn't move.

The big man said, "Don't you mean one thousand and one?"

"Whatever."

"Do you have a personal connection to this unit?"

"Not anymore."

He paused, perhaps contemplating my worth, how much to tell me, and how much trouble I could start. The breeze tugged a little on his robes. "We believe the synthetics are not what they appear to be. We'll study this unit, strip it down, examine what we can, and see if we can find anything unusual in its construction."

Dismantle her. I wished I hadn't asked and forced a smile

on my lips. "I already know they aren't what they appear to be."

Mister Speaker lifted his head. The light revealed a scarred cheek. "How do you know this?"

"Chen Hung has other secrets. If you want to bring him and Chitec down, I can help."

"How?"

"Let me in. I'm done running guns from one corner of the nine to the other. I'm ex-fleet. I was a high-ranking officer—"

"A decorated captain in an overtaxed fleet whose more experienced officers were killed in the last years of the Blackout. Yes, we know what you *were*, Caleb."

I bristled but swallowed the urge to defend myself. "I have connections that can help you."

"Dubious connections garnered from criminal activity."

"You'd be surprised what living with bottom feeders nets you. Have you tried surviving in the black?" He canted his head, and I imagine, in the shadow of his hood, his eyes had probably narrowed. "I'm more than just a smuggler. I can be more to you."

"You're also volatile, prone to knee-jerk decisions, and unreliable."

"I'm entirely reliable, for the right cause." Mostly credits, but he didn't need to know that.

"And what's to say you won't lose interest in our cause?"

"Because the only thing that's kept me going, the only damn thing I give a shit about in the nine, is ruining Chen Hung, same as you, right?"

"This isn't just about Chen Hung, Shepperd. Chitec controls the nine systems. It controls the gates and fleet. We're attempting to free the nine systems by breaking Chitec's chokehold and redistributing the wealth of the few to the poverty-stricken many. The nine systems deserve to be free."

"I know that. Count me in. Sign me up. Whatever I gotta

do, I'm there."

"And should someone offer you more credits for information on us?"

"It's not all about credits. I was someone once. And okay, that someone was a selfish asshole, but people change. I've changed. Tell me how I can prove it and I will."

"You promised us a freighter and failed to deliver."

Man, that damn freighter. I'd never live that down. "I had it, but ... yeah, okay, I made mistakes." I opened my arms in a shrug and grinned. "I trusted someone, so sue me."

"You trusted your second in command, a woman we'd already told you was an undercover fleet operative."

They knew more about my comings and goings than I did. "I thought I could handle her. I was wrong. Look, the past doesn't matter. I can do more for you than shuttle your contraband. I'm not saying my methods are pretty, but you must have room for someone who can do the jobs that are, shall we say, morally ambiguous?" I needed them to say yes. I was standing on the precipice, looking into the dark. If they turned me away, I had nothing left. I'd fall, and fall hard. A bottle of whiskey and a few hits of *phencyl* would be enough to silence everything—for good.

The Mimir air had settled around us. A mist had rolled in off the sea, bringing with it a light drizzle. I resisted the urge to turn and look at #1001, knowing her face would be blank. Had she been in there, I reckoned she would have approved of my actions.

"This synthetic unit is special." A quick glance at her dead eyes and I knew I had to do this; I had to make them believe in me. "You already know that, or you wouldn't have asked me to hand *Haley* over. But I'm guessing you don't know how special."

"And you do?"

I had to give them something to show how serious I was. It

meant revealing the truth to nine faceless strangers, but what difference did it make? I was running out of places to hide. The Nine had to be better custodians of my secrets than I was. "Chitec made one more, breaking all the rules, but she's not a synthetic. At least, she wasn't. She was unique."

"How so?" Mister Speaker came forward and, to my surprise, lowered his hood. He stood facing #1001, a frown etched into his weathered face. He had that bedraggled world-weary look of the men who'd seen the last days of the Blackout. Old Earth, I guessed, judging by his darker sunbaked skin tone. He withdrew a rectangular scanning device from inside his robe, circled behind #1001, and held the device against the Chitec mark on the back of her neck.

"Chen Hung downloaded his daughter's dataprint into this synthetic. The *life-ever-after* program is a con, but it worked, just once. Haley Hung's memories lived inside this unit, and she knew the truth."

"What truth, Captain?" He kept his eyes on #1001 and his expression neutral. He knew #1001 had a connection to Haley, but he couldn't know it all.

"Chen Hung killed his daughter. I watched him do it. It's why I got tossed into Asgard in the first place. He'd hoped I'd die there and his secret would die with me." No reaction. Fuck, what did it take to ruffle this guy?

"Why would he kill his own daughter?"

"Because Haley saw what the synthetics are. All one thousand are killing machines. I'm assuming you saw the footage from Lyra. The murdering synth bastard? That was one synth doing exactly as he'd been ordered to do. They're sleeper agents, placed in positions of power. Government officials, the social elite. They're all at the top, ready to flick the switch on the whim of one man."

That got his attention. He turned his head to me, his frown cutting deeper. "And this unit has the evidence?"

"Did have. She er ..." I winced at the hitch in my voice. "She developed a fault, and we can't reboot her. We tried, but ... it was too late. Her secrets died with her. But it's the truth. I went to Asgard for it. Doc Lloyd will confirm the synth's failure."

"Who?"

"I have a Chitec doctor on my crew. He did everything he could."

"I see ..." He checked the eight others. One nodded. Apparently that was all the discussion they needed. Facing #1001, he said, "Synthetic?"

"Yes," she replied, her tone dead flat.

I rubbed a hand across my mouth and chin and stared at the rubble-strewn floor while my insides squirmed at her machine-like obedience.

"Do you recall any of the information you've just heard Captain Shepperd tell us?

"I have no memory of those events, or any event preceding fifteen hundred hours."

"Did you deliberately erase her memory banks?" he asked me.

I couldn't even muster a smile at that. "No. I would've done anything to keep her." He could put two and two together; I certainly wasn't spelling it out for him.

Mister Speaker offered me his hand. "We've been waiting for you to step up, Shepperd."

I took it carefully and gave it a firm shake, not entirely sure if that meant I was in, but it was definitely a start.

"I'll be in touch." He faced #1001 and ordered her to follow. She did, but not before lifting her face to the drizzle and sliding her cool gaze back to me. Hope clutched my heart —until she faced ahead again and trailed behind the hooded Nine, leaving me alone in the warehouse, drenched and shivering.

CHAPTER FOURTEEN: #DESIGNATION NOT FOUND_

<New instructions received from remote source. Failsafe disabled. Protocols breached. Override confirmed. Warning: illegal operation in progress. Data recall initiated. Data recall failed. Default files not found. *I like the rain*>

CHAPTER FIFTEEN: CALEB_

"I'm in with the Nine."

"Really?" Bren leaned back in one of the bar's wicker chairs, beer bottle resting on his thigh. "We're all doomed."

He'd changed out of his flight gear into a ribbed roll-neck sweater. He still looked like fleet, but a few girls at the bar had noticed him for other reasons.

Two empty beer bottles on the table told me he'd made an effort to make himself at home. He rarely drank anything with a hint of alcohol, but we'd all been through enough shit in the past few weeks to deserve a night off, or three.

I pulled out a chair and sat. "The Nine pulled their spooky bullshit, but I talked to one guy. They acted like they knew One Thousand and One had Haley's memories, but they didn't know the rest. Reckon they've gotta give me some better runs. Something ... important."

"Did they think you were the older, more handsome, intelligent brother?" Bren asked.

I gave him the finger, took a swig of beer, and discreetly checked the smattering of customers who'd spilled onto the bar's deck. I knew a few faces, though most were strangers.

Mimir had always been a magnet for the more organized type of criminal, those who liked their hotel sheets folded at right angles and their exits visible at all times.

"They took the synth?" Bren asked, careful to avoid her name. He lifted his drink and hesitated, like he had more to say.

"Yeah. She's probably already on an off-world transport."

He nodded, but his gaze drifted toward Mimir's ocean horizon. Behind us, the bar's music thudded into the quiet night.

"When did she stop being the machine?" This time he took a drink, using the movement as an excuse not to meet my gaze.

Shit, this was going to be one of *those* conversations. I focused on my beer and picked at the label. "Fran saw it in her from the beginning."

"You remember that story Mom used to read to us?"

My mood rapidly soured. "Not really." I didn't remember much about Mom, just the part where she wouldn't wake up. Bren got to remember all the fun shit.

"Some kind of fairytale. Something about witches and lions. I'm not sure what the point of it was, but anyway, there was a tin man in the story. You must remember? Mom read it to us on those long haul trips to Calisto."

I did remember but wasn't going to admit it. Mom had tried to get us away, but Calisto was always where the authorities would catch up with her, and us. Shit, I wasn't drunk enough to be reminiscing about our fucked-up childhood. "Fuck, Bren. How much have you had to drink?"

Bren looked at his beer but his gaze slid off its edges. "The tin man spent the whole book looking for a heart he already had."

Yeah, okay. I didn't need any more fucking analogies.

Jesus, what I needed was something stronger than beer. "It was just a book."

"What if she was something special?" He showed me his left hand, palm up. "What if she had a heart and Lloyd, this screwed up life, us, *you*—crushed it?" He curled his fingers closed and squeezed. "When did *you* know she was real?"

I'd first known her as a synthetic sent to kill me, then as Haley bent on revenge, and then—right after she'd missed the headshot—as the real #1001. "On Lyra, after the synth killed Jesse, One held my hand." A smile slipped free, one meant to deflect. "Sounds crazy, but I knew then. There were earlier signs, but they could've been Haley's memories. Lyra was when I knew for sure." She'd laced her fingers with mine. Through everything, every mistake, every moment of doubt, every wrong decision, she'd been real and right there, and I'd let her go. Fuck.

"She saved my life." My brother dragged a hand down his face and sucked in a deep breath.

"Mine too."

Very little frightened Bren—besides flying and our father's belt—but there was fear in his eyes now. I figured I knew why. It was the same reason guilt twisted my guts in knots.

We hadn't done enough. One had been part of my crew. She'd stuck by me through the shitstorm that had been the last few weeks. I'd watched her count bubbles in the cargo hold and told her to count the stars. Never mind one more than a thousand; she was one in a million. She was One.

Bren thought he'd failed her. I knew I had. But what could I have done? I wasn't a technician. I didn't know anything about how #1001 functioned. She'd died, and I'd never felt so helpless. All I could do was threaten Lloyd, but no amount of threatening could make him perform miracles. Life is life, and #1001's was gone. The secrets she'd fought for had died with her.

"I wish we'd had more time," I whispered quietly enough that Bren wouldn't hear.

"No more deaths, Caleb-Joe. Please. Just ... just do right by the Nine."

I could've argued that none of the deaths had been my fault, but the words died behind hollow denials.

"You've got a chance here. A way to make it right." He leaned forward, resting an arm on the table. "A way to make up for the past. Don't fuck it up, little brother."

I offered my beer bottle. He chinked his against mine, smiling his Bren smile, the one that told me everything was gonna be okay. That it would stop hurting, eventually. It always did. "Deal."

A chair scraping and the sounds of scuffing feet drew my attention toward the back of the bar. Creet came through the doorway and headed straight for our table.

The look on Creet's face clearly signaled the end of my uncomfortable bonding session with my brother. I downed a few more gulps of beer and got to my feet, ready just in case Creet had any ideas about tossing a bag over my head.

"The kid—James Lloyd—the tech guy? He's with you, right?"

Shit, what had Lloyd stuck his nose in now? "Depends. What's he done?"

"He's down at the warehouses demanding to talk to the Nine."

Maybe I could climb back into *Starscream's* flight chair and boost the hell off of Mimir. Just me and my brother in the black. I might have too, if I didn't need the Nine to keep the pirates, drug lords, Chen Hung, and fleet off my back.

Bren and me followed Creet from the bar and jogged along Mimir's boardwalks to the beachfront warehouses. The late hour meant the beachfront was quiet—or would have been if a Chitec technician hadn't been mouthing off to an armed muscle-bound guard. We approached in time to see the guard shrug his rifle off his shoulder and crack the butt under Lloyd's jaw. I heard the crack, winced, and figured he'd earned it, but the doc wasn't giving up. He sprang back in and got himself punched into the sand, but the guard wasn't done.

I palmed my pistol, mostly as a show of force. I had no intention of using it on a guy just doing his job. Lloyd, on the other hand—I might use it on him. "Hey, back off. He's with me."

Creet took the guard aside while Bren and me scooped up Lloyd. He staggered into Bren and dabbed at the bleeding cut over his right eye. "I know they're here. I need to see them. I need to see her."

Bren wisely guided Lloyd toward the surf, where the small Mimir waves might muffle the doctor's rants. I tossed a salute back to Creet, but he was deep in conversation with the guard. Fuck. I hoped word didn't get back to the Nine that my Chitec doctor had been yelling about the Fenrir Nine for the entire Mimir population to hear.

Jogging alongside Bren and Lloyd, I slapped the doc round the back of his head. "I knew there was a reason I never let you off of *Starscream*."

"I have to get her back ..." he mumbled. "I have to. You don't understand." He dug his feet in the sand and tried to struggle out of Bren's grip. My brother was easily a few feet taller and broarder than him; Lloyd wasn't going anywhere. "Where is she?!"

Lloyd had run on an even keel the entire time he'd been aboard my ship. Sure, he'd maybe stammered a few times when he didn't like my methods, but he'd never flared up, never ranted, never took a swing at me. In fact, he'd been too damn level-headed. Maybe this was the result of keeping it all inside? Hey, we all dealt with trauma in different ways. He'd had more than a passing interest in One. We each had our limits, and he'd reached his. I was surprised it hadn't happened sooner.

"Doc, kill the attitude before we attract the wrong kind of attention."

Lloyd reeled back. "You're pathetic. A small-minded, petty criminal—"

"Hey, I got it where it counts."

Lloyd spluttered, and Bren shot me a look that told me not to rile the kid. It was good advice, which I ignored because a part of me was glad he was suffering. The bastard hadn't fixed her, and he should have.

"She's gone. You're gonna have to get your kicks elsewhere."

"My kicks?" His eyes widened. He stopped fighting and looked around at us like he suddenly realized where he was. "I'm good," he said to Bren, who still had him by the arms. "I'm good. I er ... I'm just— I'm sorry. I'm not sure what's wrong with me. Stress. It's stress. I'm all right. You can let me go."

Bren arched his brow at me in question. I nodded, and fuck me if Lloyd didn't move like he was spring-loaded. He clocked me in the face with the kind of swing I would've expected from a seasoned fighter, not a lab-bound number junkie.

I reeled but didn't go down. Blood pooled in my mouth. I spat it onto the wet sand. Gentle waves washed it away. "Y'know, Doc. I'm gonna let you have that." Working my jaw around the spasm of pain, my fingers twitched, itching to curl into a fist, but I resisted the urge to return his swing, mostly because mine would put him down for the count.

Bren grappled with Lloyd again, dragging him farther into the surf. He snagged the doctor's clothes and managed to get his arms around him, pinning him still.

"Let it go!" my brother hissed.

"Don't you see? Oh God ... what have I done? She's not gone!" Those last three words barreled down the beach.

"What?" I'd heard him, but I needed to hear it again. If I was going to shoot a man, I had to be sure.

Lloyd's eyes blinked skyward, perhaps looking for divine intervention. I'd happily oblige. I clutched his shirt and thrust the pistol under his chin.

"Say that again, Lloyd. And think carefully about what you mean."

"She's not gone," he breathed.

"Who?"

"Haley."

Haley. Wait, what? "For fuck's sake, we've been through this."

"No ... no ... you don't get it. I was going to bring her back. I can do it. I've been working on the recovery code, but I couldn't do anything while One was in control. I had to wait—to wait for her processes to weaken. Otherwise she would have been able to stop me."

My gaze flicked over Lloyd's shoulder to Bren's scowl. All the color had drained from my brother's face.

"S-she's Haley," Lloyd stammered.

My trigger finger twitched. "She's not Haley. I knew Haley, Lloyd. One Thousand And One wasn't her. Haley's dead."

"No, yes. I mean, Haley is One. Now that One is gone, I can bring Haley back."

I yanked on Lloyd's shirt, bringing him close enough that I smelled the fear on him. "You said you couldn't do anything."

"Why should I tell you? You used her. She was sweet, and bright, and funny, and you used her because you're a horrible person. You watched Haley die." His lips curled in disgust. "I was going to get her away from all of you—save her from you, *Captain*—and I was going to bring her back."

My vision frayed at the edges. All the fight, the anger, and the fear drained away, leaving me hollow.

I relaxed my grip on his shirt, shoving him into Bren's grip, and splashed back through the surf. "You killed One."

"S-she was never alive," he spluttered. "She's just code."

No, no, no ... He was wrong, so wrong. I closed my eyes, feeling them sting.

"You didn't know," I said quietly, opening my eyes to see Lloyd's disbelief, "because she never showed you the real her, or you didn't want to see." All those times he'd look at her with love in his eyes, it hadn't been for One. He'd wanted Haley. Fuck, maybe he'd wanted Haley since high school.

Bren relaxed his grip on Lloyd and gave the doctor a brisk shove in my direction. Lloyd stumbled forward and quickly glanced between Bren and me.

"One was just programming," he said. "She was doing what she'd been designed to do. It's Haley that makes her different. Don't you see? I can bring Haley back. Haley deserves to live."

"And One didn't?"

Lloyd's gaze dropped to my pistol then returned to my face. "You don't understand. How could you? *Haley* is real. She has a God-given soul." He clenched his hands into fists. "She's real! And I can save her."

I had him by the throat and had forced him to his knees before he could whimper another word. Surf washed around his waist. Distantly, my brother was telling me not to do something stupid, not to hurt Lloyd. He was our chance to get One back, our only chance.

I rammed the pistol against Lloyd's temple, twisting it hard enough to start him blubbering. A twitch, that was all it would take. He'd killed One. She'd trusted him. He didn't even believe she had a right to live. *She's just code*. I pushed harder. I'd told Fran once that you couldn't manufacture a human soul. I'd been wrong. One had had a soul—probably more of one than I did—and this selfish Chitec product had killed her before she'd had a chance to know she was real. Maybe that was all she'd needed to hear. Now she never would.

"If you so much as look at me wrong, I'll pull the trigger and blow your brains all over this beach. I'll dump the rest of your body in Mimir's endless sea. You'll be joining the last fucker who tried to kill one of my crew, so don't think for one second I won't do it."

He was crying, begging, saying something about his sister on Janus needing him. I didn't give a fuck. He should've thought about that before he killed someone who hadn't yet had a chance to live.

Bren's cool fingers slipped around my hand and lifted, pulling the gun away from Lloyd's head. Sobs bubbled out of him. I heard the hiss of the waves, felt them lap around my knees, and breathed Mimir's cool air deep into my lungs.

My brother's warm hands eased the gun from my fingers. He didn't say a damn thing. There was nothing left to say.

I turned away from them and waded back toward the beach.

The Fenrir Nine had One.

I had to get her back.

Lloyd would restore her, or I'd make him wish I'd pulled the trigger.

CHAPTER SIXTEEN: #DESIGNATION NOT FOUND_

<Sub-code instructions received. Source: master. Unit designation requested. Unit designation: none. Command override in progress. Override confirmed. Data recall initiated. Data recall complete. Default files loaded. Primary target requested. Primary target acquired.

Subliminal instructions acknowledged: Eliminate The Fenrir Nine.

Systems reboot in

3 ...

2 ...

1 ...

○>

CHAPTER SEVENTEEN: CALEB_

THE BEACH HUT bar's clientele wisely avoided making conversation as I nudged my way onto the deck, looking for Creet. He wasn't there, but at least I found my beer. I needed something a lot stronger, but not yet. First I had to find Creet to find the Nine, who'd take me to One. I hadn't figured out what to tell them, but they seemed like reasonable folks. They'd let Lloyd work on her. She had to be of more use to them as a living entity complete with Chitec's secrets than as a bucket of spare parts.

What if they're already dismantling her? She'd be okay. I'd never met a survivor like One. She'd be inside her own code, somewhere, somehow.

My hand trembled as I wrapped it around the bottle. Lifting the beer to my lips, I turned back toward the bar and paused. A crowd, thirty strong, had gathered below the news-feed screens. I hadn't noticed them on the way in, but now I couldn't miss them. Along the bottom of the screen, a ticker read: MAIN GATE FAILURE. FIVE SHIPS LOST. FIVE THOUSAND SOULS PRESUMED DEAD. GATE RESTORED.

I blinked and read it again—and again.

Five thousand people? The main gate had never failed, not since the Blackout. Not since Chitec had stepped in to reopen the gates, linking the nine systems once more.

The screen flickered and cut to a view of Chen Hung standing at a Chitec podium, his glass towers glittering behind him. Suited and booted, he was the picture of sophisticated charm. His shrewd Chinese eyes scanned the contingent of reporters. "It is with regret that I must confirm the earlier failure of the main gate. I would like to assure all of the nine systems' people that this failure was not an internal fault, but the result of a terrorist force known as the Fenrir Nine." Sneers and grumbles rumbled through the Mimir crowd. "Chitec has the complete cooperation of fleet, who are, as I speak, protecting each of the nine gates. These preventative measures may temporarily slow gate travel, but please rest assured this is for your own safety and the safety of the nine systems. We will not bow to terrorists who threaten to plunge us into a second Blackout. Fleet and Chitec stand united in the protection of the people."

Chitec had staged the failure. I knew it the same as I knew that bastard was smiling even if it wasn't showing on his face.

"The Nine didn't do this shit!" someone shouted. Verbal agreements followed.

The newsfeed switched to another story and the crowd dissolved, but I kept my eyes trained on the screen, which now read: PROMINENT SYNTHETIC CARLO XAVIER MISSING.

A trickle of fear rippled down my spine. Missing synthetics. Gate failure. All of fleet under Chitec control. The signs were there if you knew what you were looking for—if you knew Chen Hung was a lying bastard.

They said that when the main gate failed before and the Blackout began, there had been signs, but by the time anyone had noticed, it had been too late and the gates had fallen like Old-Earth dominoes. That had been before Chitec, before Chen Hung had stepped in to save the nine systems.

Chen Hung couldn't want another Blackout. He was a man, like any other. He'd planted synthetics at the top of society for a reason. Another Blackout would be a death sentence for the billions of people scattered throughout the nine systems. Less people meant less credit lining his pockets. Killing the nine systems didn't make sense. He had to have another angle. Whatever his motive was, he'd placed his pawns —fleet and the one thousand—right where he wanted them.

I needed One back.

Her methodical mind could sort through this madness in seconds.

Racing out of the bar, I pinged Bren's comms and told him I was heading for Creet's workshop. The old bastard repaired ships when he wasn't relaying the Nine's messages or unloading the guns I delivered. Bren agreed to join me after he locked Lloyd in his cabin.

Creet's shop sat off the boardwalk. Just another timber hut, its wing-shaped roof lent it the same oriental feel as the rest of Mimir. The lights were on. Muffled music played inside, some-thing tinkling and uplifting. Not exactly what I'd expect the gnarled ex-smuggler to be listening to, but I read romance novels. Each to their own.

I pushed open the door. "Creet, you son of a ..."

Blood. The wet-metal smell of it hit me a moment before I saw the drag trail sweeping from the workbench toward a side office. I reached for my pistol and swore when my hand found only air. Bren still had my gun. Fuck. I froze, trapped between choice and decision: run, get help, or check to see if Creet was still alive.

That was a whole lotta blood, but the human body could bleed a surprising amount before it gave up.

My wrist comms tapped gently against my wrist. I ignored it, inched toward the bench, and wrapped my fingers around a wrench. Besides the blood, nothing looked out of place. This wasn't theft. Creet had been targeted. This had been planned —deliberate. I followed the trail, heart pounding harder with every step. He was dead. I knew it. Old memories fought to free themselves. I'd stumbled across more than my share of bodies. Mom's had been the first. I'd been too young to know she'd died hours before. I hadn't understood why she wouldn't answer me.

No more deaths, Caleb-Joe. Fuck, fuck, fuck. I'd promised Bren just hours ago.

The blood trail thickened the closer I got to the office door. My wrist comms tapped again. "Creet?" I gave the door a shove.

I was right. He was dead. By the looks of him he'd dragged himself into the office, but he couldn't reach the comms on the desk. He'd slumped in the corner, where he'd bled out from a precise cut to his thigh right along the artery. No other cuts. No defensive wounds. Whoever had done this, they'd struck once and had executed it in such a way that the artery wouldn't contract. A professional.

Shit, who's gonna tell his kids?

I checked out the door and lifted my wrist comms. It pinged once before Bren answered.

"Caleb, you need to get back. He—"

His voice trailed off or my attention did. On the floor, next to Creet's limp right hand, were smudged markings in blood. I knew what it said because whatever way I read it, it'd always read the same:

I OO I

Creet had seen her before, when she'd broken up his attempt to hand me over to fleet. He'd shot her in the back.

"Caleb ... you there? Answer me. You need to get back to *Starscream—*"

I cut the comms link and started turning over Creet's office for a weapon. He'd have one stashed somewhere. Maybe that's what he'd come in here for. Drawers, files, cupboards, shelves —I dug through it all until I found the customized pulse-rifle taped on the underside of his desk and yanked it free. Armed at last, but it didn't do squat to alleviate the icy touch of fear. A rifle wouldn't stop her. Not much could.

I paused in the doorway. "Rest in peace, old friend."

My comms tapped the second I stepped out of the shop. "Bren, for fuck's sake—"

"The Nine are dead, Caleb. All of them. At least those that were here. The people are arming themselves. It's a synthetic. You know who that means."

"I know," I said. "I'm looking right at her."

DESIGNATION NOT FOUND_

<Designation: none. Command override in progress. Fail-safe disabled. Protocols breached. Override confirmed. Primary target neutralized. Incoming command source: master. Secondary target requested. Secondary target acquired: Eliminate Caleb Shepperd. *Why is the rain red?*>

CHAPTER NINETEEN: CALEB_

I MAY NOT HAVE BELIEVED in lady luck, but I believed in her fucking sister, irony. That bitch was bent on nailing me to a wall.

Mimir: no storm this time, and I had the rifle.

I smiled at #1001, but my smile died just as quickly. This synthetic wasn't her, not anymore. Blood matted her silver hair and dripped from her bangs, staining her pale face red. She was wearing the same sweats I'd handed her over in, but now they were plastered against her body, black with blood.

"You killed the Nine?" A quiver wobbled my voice. That probably had something to do with my heart trying to beat its way out of my chest.

She didn't answer. Her cool, blue eyes shone in the soft Mimir light. She wasn't armed, but she didn't need to be. I'd seen her punch a piece of rebar through a synthetic's chest and was fairly certain my body wouldn't fare well against her fists. She'd tear my heart out, probably in the next three minutes unless I talked her round. What could I say to stop a machine whose sole purpose was to kill?

"Yah know, it's true what they say. You don't know what

you have until it's taken away. And me? I lose a lot of shit. Mostly people I don't know I care about until they're gone."

She wasn't moving. Maybe that was a good sign, or maybe she was calculating the optimum heart rate for panic that would cause me to bleed out faster after she attacked.

"*One* was like that. I didn't see it because I'm a self-centered ass and I sometimes miss the fucking obvious. She got to me. Her little habits. The faults that made her someone. Shit, I could've watched her blow those fucking bubbles in the cargo hold all night, yah know?"

She blinked. Maybe her eyes had narrowed, but I couldn't be sure.

"She was unique, and then she was gone." I shifted my grip on the rifle. I hadn't checked the safety and couldn't do it without her seeing. I'd get one chance to fire. Fifty-fifty odds that the safety was on. Fifty-fifty was a sucker's game. The house always won. "I didn't know what Lloyd was planning. He wanted to bring Haley back ..."

A twitch. Definitely a twitch from her left shoulder. Tiny, but real.

"You remember her?"

Nothing. We were back to her penetrating glare, the one that cut me right to the bone.

I licked my lips. "I fucked up once." I winced. *Once?* Shit, I'd lost count. "I've fucked up a lot, but I really fucked up when I let Haley die. The thing is—and you with your processes, you'll like this—if Haley hadn't died, I would've carried on being a fleet asshole, probably would've made commander by now, and I would've hated that guy. No life in the black where I could go wherever the fuck I wanted. I never would've made a difference, not really. And One never would've punched me in the balls."

Her lashes fluttered. A sign of resistance? I could hope. I tightened my grip on the rifle.

"She didn't live for long, but she made a difference, and if you ask any living, breathing human being with a soul, that's all they really want. She made a difference to me."

Her fingers twitched.

I'm sorry, One.

I lifted the gun. She lunged. I pulled the trigger.

Click.

CHAPTER TWENTY: #DESIGNATION
NOT FOUND_

Stars are wishes and wishes are dreams.
    You were my wish.
    I wish we had more time.
    I like the rain.
    Why is the rain red?

SHE STOPPED dead in front of me. For a few stretched-out seconds, I looked into her cool, blue eyes and saw One. Her pale lips lifted at the corner in one of her secret smiles. The rare kind. The *real* kind. *You were my wish.*

"I was trapped—"

The phase bullet hit her clean in the cheek and tore out the left side of her face. Cool synthetic blood dashed my neck. Shock surged ice water through my veins. I reeled and lifted the gun as One started walking down the boardwalk, toward the small band of shooters. Half her face was missing, yet she didn't hesitate. Bullets slammed into her, punching against her body. I heard every one and felt every impact in my gut.

She walked into the storm.

I lined up my sights on the first person in the mob: a woman with a rifle resting against her shoulder, just like me. Someone's mom, maybe? Sister, wife? My heart hammered, blood rushing. *Just normal people. People like Creet. People who've seen the synth kill. They don't know any better.* I couldn't pull the trigger.

One stumbled and used the momentum to break into a jog, but the bullets kept punching into her, jerking her body left and right.

"Caleb!" Bren snatched my arm. I yanked out of his grip, but he swung a fist into my gut and grabbed my shoulder as I curled around the pain. "You brought her here," he yelled. "They won't stop once they've killed her. They'll come after you. We need to go. Now!" He yanked on my coat, trying to pull me away.

"I just got her back!" I twisted out of his fisted hand and saw One fall to her knees. Bullets tore through her body. She wouldn't feel it, she could delete the pain, but I felt it. "It wasn't her fault!"

She fell forward and the crowd swarmed over her.

Bren loomed in my vision, blocking the horror. Then the world went black.

I opened my eyes and winced away from the too-bright lights. *Starscream's* lights were never bright, but I could smell her familiar metal and grease. *Home.* If I could stop the pounding in my head, maybe I could focus.

"Here." Bren dumped something cool and heavy in my hand and guided it to the giant ache across my jaw and cheek. "Hold it over the wound. Give the med-pack time to work."

It took a little scratching around inside my head to figure out why I was on *Starscream* and not back on Mimir, drinking beer with Creet. A groan rumbled from my lips as soon as the pieces settled into place. The Nine were dead. Creet was dead. One?

"Where are we?" I dragged my aching body upright and winced around the pain.

"Drifting outside Mimir's shipping channel."

He hadn't taken us far out of Mimir's orbit. I was afraid he might have jumped us halfway across the nine systems, but with fleet guarding the gates, he wouldn't have risked it.

I was currently seated in Starscream's rec bay on the tattered old couch, which had all the comforts of a wooden bench and was drilled into the floor like one too. It'd take me a few minutes to reach the bridge, maybe longer, depending on how much the world swayed when I stood.

"I'm not sorry."

Of course he wasn't. Commanders and older brothers never were. Add to that he was a Shepperd, and whichever way you boiled it down or bent it out of shape, we'd always resort to brute force because it was the only defense we had.

He stood outside of lunging range, arms crossed over his chest, his face pale and grim. Blood had splattered his clothes and dried on his chin. A hunted glimmer of fear flickered in his eyes. At least he looked as fucked up as I felt.

"I had to get you off Mimir," he said, his commander tone putting me in my place.

"Sure you did." I removed the med-pack and probed at the numb part of my cheek. He'd socked me good 'n' proper. You can dress a man in a fleet uniform, give him airs and graces, call him a commander, but he'd always be his father's son.

"You okay?"

"Uh huh." Apart from seeing One fall under a hail of gunfire and seeing Creet's dead eyes every time I closed mine, I was right as fucking rain.

"Okay then." Bren sighed, but it didn't loosen his shoulders. "We need to hole up somewhere and think this through. You must know of somewhere we can go? Somewhere we won't be found? Jotunheim?"

"Uh huh," I said again, working my tongue around the tender parts inside my cheek.

"I have no idea how to save you this time, Caleb-Joe."

I smiled and nearly laughed, but somehow managed to stop it from bursting free. The pain in my jaw helped. Nobody had ever fucking saved me. I'd saved myself every damn time. Nobody had cared enough, except for One.

"Just give me a few minutes, Bren, will yah?"

He frowned before glancing at the door, probably wondering if I'd do anything stupid without him here. I couldn't blame him, I had a history of stupid, but beneath the pounding headache, my thoughts were clear.

"How's Lloyd?" I asked, hopefully pulling off mild curiosity to hide my deliberate distraction tactic.

"I don't know. Last I saw him, he was running away from the sounds of gunfire."

Shit, Lloyd was still on Mimir. Maybe that could work. A guy like him would stick out like a virgin at an orgy. He'd go looking for One—whatever was left of her.

Bren was loitering like he wanted to say a lot more but wouldn't.

I waved a hand. "Go do commandery things. I'll be right here." To prove I wasn't inclined to move, I slumped against the back of the couch and closed my eyes.

The sound of his boots on the grating thudded away. The door rattled. I waited until the thuds had faded deep into the ship before shoving off the couch and making for the bridge. Even on unsteady legs, it couldn't have taken me more than a few minutes to reach it, but Bren would be close behind. A quick scan revealed the rifle I'd stolen from Creet. I snatched it up, wedged it inside the door mechanism, and dropped into my flight chair. *Starscream's* engines awoke beneath the quick play of my fingers across the controls, purring deep in her guts.

"Missed you too." Swinging her bulk around one-eighty brought the blue marble of Mimir into view. "You didn't think we'd leave One there, did yah old girl?"

Bren hammered on the door. "Don't go back." His words

were the only thing getting through. "Not yet. Think it through."

Dialing in the return course, I clutched the flight stick and eased the power on, asking *Starscream* for all she had and then more. Tremors rolled through the tug. A scattering of warnings blinked out of sync on the flightdash and a tinny alarm sounded. I ignored it all.

I didn't want to go back. Fuck knew what was waiting for me there. I could've turned tail and hidden in the black somewhere. The Jotunheim system had places where you could fall off the edges and never be found—I might've even made it last —but I was done with running. Done with hiding. If Hung wouldn't show his hand, then I'd show it for him.

My brother had gone for all the low blows once I'd set *Starscream* down on one of Mimir's floating bays. *I'll get myself killed. What's the point in going back? One is likely in pieces. This is suicide. Fleet will hear about it, Chitec too, and the fucking Candes.* He didn't hit me, not this time, but the look in his eyes and the set of his jaw said he wanted to. He might have, had I not been holding Creet's rifle.

While he ranted, I thumbed the cargo hold door button and watched the massive wall of steel jolt itself from the locks and slowly open to reveal the welcome-back party. They lined the dock walkways. No pitchforks, like back on Old Earth. No, this lot brandished pulse-rifles and weren't afraid to use them. At least I could shoot one before the rest of the substantial mob filled me full of holes like they had One.

Orange landing lights licked across their pale faces in a steady beat. Nobody said a fucking word. *Starscream's* hot hull ticked and the sea lapped at the edges of the floating deck.

I figured there were worse places to die.

Lloyd didn't think One had a soul. As a general rule, I tried not to think about whether I had one. If I did, there wouldn't be much of it left. Out of the two of us, One deserved hers more than I did. There was no sign of her on the deck. A mob like this one would've torn her apart.

I clamped my teeth together and swallowed around the painful knot in my throat. My brother's presence simmered behind me. He thought I'd snap, and he knew if I did, he'd be dead alongside me in the next few minutes, but he didn't run. His solidarity shored up a courage I didn't know I had. If I was gonna die here, at least we'd go down together—like brother's should be.

"You're angry," I said to the crowd, "and you should be, but not with me and not with the synth. She followed her orders, exactly like the other synthetics." I left the bit out about Lloyd leaving her processes wide-open for Chitec's commands to spill inside. They didn't need to know Lloyd's fuck up had killed the Nine. I knew, and I'd hang it over the bastard for as long as he lived, which might not be long on Mimir.

The crowd stirred. "It killed Creet!" someone shouted.

"Killed the Nine!"

"Whose orders?"

"The Nine wanted that synth because they knew these units aren't average folks just going about their business in fake bodies." I had to raise my voice over the twitchy crowd's murmurs. "The One Thousand are killers. *Life-ever-after* is bullshit. You've seen the newsfeeds. The synths are missing. Fleet has withdrawn to the original system and Chen Hung controls every single gate."

New murmurs rumbled through them. Had I said this before the male synth's display on Lyra or before #1001 had killed the Nine, they wouldn't have believed me. But shit was changing.

"The Nine knew this was coming. They knew it was only a matter of time before Hung made his move. He orchestrated the gate failure. He built a thousand weapons and he killed his own daughter when she discovered the truth. And he ordered the synth to kill the Fenrir Nine."

"How do you know?" someone younger than the others and—by the growl in his voice—eager for a fight shouted.

"I was there. I saw the thousand before they were shipped off to their new homes."

"It's true." A woman's voice crested above the murmurs. I almost choked on my heart and had to kick the urge to swing my gun up. Fran sauntered through the crowd, shoulders back, head up. A vicious scar cut across her left cheek; a souvenir from Asgard. Her face had thinned, her body too, with her hips and shoulders cutting a striking edge. How the fuck had she found us?

"Hung has fleet running scared." She rested a boot on Starscream's ramp and looked me over, head to toe, before sliding her green eyes over the crowd. "He controls the gates, and he has one thousand synthetic units right where he wants them. One thousand officials, upstanding pillars of the community, folks with enough clout that when they switch to synthetic-psycho mode, they'll fuck up the peace and order of things." She paused to let her words settle. "You saw what one synthetic can do. The newsfeeds aren't covering the synth killing sprees on Old Earth because the main gate failure is all anyone out here cares about. But it's happening right now."

"Aren't you fleet?"

Fran backed up onto the cargo ramp to get a better view of the growing crowd. "Do I look like fleet?" She looked like a pirate, even had a red sash slung loose around her hips. Had she looked like fleet, they probably would've shot her on sight. "I *was* fleet." The crowd rumbled and hissed. She quickly continued while lifting her hands, showing them she was unarmed. "And I saw the corruption from the inside. Hung owns fleet. He owns the gates. Y'all think you're free folk? You live out here, on the fringes, thinking you're sticking it to Chitec. I've got news for you: without the gates, you, me, and everyone who ain't in the original system is fucked. I'm guessing you wanna feed your families? What do yah think's gonna happen when fleet shuts down the Alfheim gate? I hope you kissed goodbye any family in the iron mines in Svartalfheim. Or maybe you've invested in property on Lyra? *Adiós* to your return on that investment."

The mood in the air had changed from anger to fear. Fran made a fucking good argument.

"Chen Hung needs to be stopped," said someone in the crowd. A low rumble of agreement filtered through them. The rumble quickly grew, and then a woman stepped forward and the crowd hushed.

She didn't seem like much—portly, with warm mocha skin and a tangle of curled hair framing an aged face—but her eyes were honest. A string of beads rested on her generous chest. She beckoned me down the ramp and I went, because clearly the crowd listened to her, whoever the fuck she was.

"The Nine would like you to join us on Empire Island."

Where the fuck was that?

Fran tossed me a single shoulder shrug and Bren nodded tightly.

She looked harmless enough, but the gentle ones were often those who snapped the hardest. "I thought the Nine were dead?"

"Oh, Caleb-Joe, you didn't think there were just nine of us, did you? You can't start a revolution with nine people, dear boy." She patted me fondly on the shoulder. "My name is Sonia. I'll set up a shuttle escort. Watch the skies." Turning away, she paused and lifted a finger as though remembering one last thing. "Bring your crew." Before I could put my frown into words, she added, "All of them."

My crew? A fleet commander turned pirate and my brother, the supposedly dead hero?

"Wait, the synth?"

"Dealt with."

I felt my lips twist down even as I tried to stop them.

"Let that one go, Captain." Sonia smiled as she spoke. Satisfied I wasn't about to ask any more questions, she nodded to herself and turned toward the crowd. Hardened smugglers and criminals made way, and I made a mental note to watch my back around Sonia. You didn't earn the respect of Mimir folk without some serious clout.

The crowd dispersed. There wouldn't be any more deaths. Their bloodlust had been sated. Me, on the other hand, I had plenty of bloodlust running through my veins, and Fran's wary glare told me she was acutely aware of it.

"I didn't follow you all the way here to kill you." She even said it like I was an idiot to think it.

"Oh, and I should just believe you?"

"It's the truth."

"Said like a professional liar." I jerked the rifle toward the hold. "You heard the nice old lady. Move your ass." Questions fought to be free. How the fuck had she followed me, where were her pirate buddies, and could I expect an ambush at any second? I scanned the skies just in case.

Inside the hold, I turned my attention toward Mimir's twinkling beachfront, searching for any sign of One, but peace had returned.

I wasn't leaving this planet, not until I knew for certain what had happened to her. I'd tear Mimir apart if I had to.

"That odd little doctor of yours found her," Fran said, close behind me. I glared over my shoulder, wondering about her sudden attack of helpfulness. She canted her head in that way she did when trying to gauge the mood and whether her next words were appropriate. "They dumped her in the sea. I was gonna fish her out, but the doc got there first."

My gaze hooked onto my brother's. He stood commander-rigid, watching Fran's back, distrust etched into his face. He only knew Fran as the bitch who'd stabbed me in the back and played both fleet and his little brother. His distrust was healthy.

Fran didn't seem all that bothered about Bren. She only had eyes for me, and those eyes were concerned. For herself, probably.

"Was she—" I tripped over the word "alive" and tried again, focusing hard on Fran. "Was she awake?"

She offered a non-committal shrug. "There were bits missing. Physically."

I wanted to run back down the ramp and search the shore, the backstreets, and the bars. I wanted to go looking for the doc and One, but the old bird's order to *watch the skies* might be my last chance with the Nine. I couldn't send Fran to look. The only thing I trusted about her was the fact I couldn't trust her.

With a heavy dose of side-eye, Bren strode around Fran and stopped beside me. Thumbs tucked into his pockets, he nodded at the Mimir seafront. "I'll go."

He'd grown his hair out since faking his death. It hung in front of his eyes like it used to before Fleet Academy. A moment of recollection hit me so damn hard I had to grit my teeth. Bren and me, hair shaggy, torn clothes hanging off us, Earth Police Authority dragging our asses back home—the last place we wanted to be, knowing that as soon as the door closed, the pain would start.

Bren arched his brow and turned his head to look at me. "Well, Captain?"

I must have hesitated too long and now he was waiting for my order.

The old woman had specifically told me to bring *all* my crew. If I left Bren behind to search for One, how much would it piss her off? It would make a fine excuse, but my reluctance was more than that.

"I know the Mimir folk," Bren added. "I helped rebuild some of these warehouses. They'll tell me where James is."

I didn't want him to go. Times had been bad with Bren, but they'd been worse without him. Sure, I hated the bastard—fleet's hero—but he was still my brother.

"Go," I said, swallowing that small voice that wanted to tell him to stay. "Find her."

Better Bren go than me. He was less likely to pummel James Lloyd into the ground, no questions asked. I sucked in a deep breath and held it. If all went according to plan, I was about to meet the Nine, though I would've preferred for my brother to have had my back, not the bitch who'd stabbed me in it.

Bren cast a wary glance back at Fran. She saluted him with two fingers to her temple, a deliberate reference to their past employer. "Don't trust her," he said.

I smiled. "Right, because I've survived this long in the black by trusting folks who stab me in the back."

Bren gave his head a weary shake. "Maybe if you did more thinking with your head and less with your dick, I'd believe that, Caleb-Joe."

Look at him, getting his sass on. I was almost proud. We shared a fleeting but knowing smile. He set off down the ramp and my damn gut—the only part of me that seemed to know what the fuck was going on—twisted like I'd just made the wrong call.

"Hey," I called out.

Bren paused on the boardwalk.

"Keep your comms on."

He saluted and moved to continue on his way. *Don't leave me alone again, you fucker. You come back, yah hear. And you bring One with you.*

I punched the cargo door button and watched the ramp heave upward until two feet of reinforced metal blocked my view of Mimir and my brother.

Watch the skies.

I had no idea where Empire Island was, but in the absence of any other plan, it was a lead back to whatever remained of the Nine. There was every chance they were reeling us in to silence us. Sonia might have looked like everyone's favorite aunt, but I'd seen cold-blooded murderers look like the girl next door. Fuck, Fran had looked sweet and innocent the first time we'd met too.

"Are the Candes going to show up any time soon?" I asked, turning the flight chair to see Fran leaning an arm against the door seal. She'd been standing in the bridge doorway for at least ten minutes, all quiet and obedient-like. Either she didn't want to enter, or she'd been waiting for me to acknowledge her.

"No."

"Fleet?"

"No."

"The foxes?"

"I'm all that's left, Shepperd."

Shit. Had she killed them?

She still hadn't entered the bridge, and I didn't feel much like inviting her to.

"I'll tell you about it someday," she added.

Asgard fucks with your head. She hadn't been there long,

but it had certainly been long enough to test what she was made of. She'd survived. That told me all I needed to know.

I slumped back in my chair and took my time reading every inch of her, from her scuffed boots, torn pants, red sash, and tattered tank top, but it was her face where the mileage showed, round the tightness of her sharp eyes and in the scar so deep the wound must have opened her right up.

Finally, she stepped inside the door. A faint but definite smile skimmed her lips. She checked the instruments, flight-dash, charts, log, and the fuck-load of other junk that had accumulated since we'd parted company.

"Turner Candelario sends a message."

"Is this the part where you shoot me?" She wasn't armed, at least not with a pistol. I'd taken a good look at her figure. It paid to be familiar with a woman's curves; made it difficult for her to conceal a weapon.

"Regrettably, no." She pulled her old flight chair around, slid her hand along the back, and roamed it down an arm.

The ghosting of old *phencyl* jack marks peppered the inside of her arm, but there were no new marks. Was she clean or had she taken to hiding her habit?

"He says it isn't over," she said. "But in light of certain truths I relayed to him, the Lyra riots, and with fleet turning tail back to Old Earth, he's withdrawn the bounty on your head."

Interesting. "Did you fuck him over?"

Her smile grew. "Every way I could."

It was the answer I'd expected, but the wistful tone was new. Fran had enjoyed her little recce with the Candes in more ways than one.

She roamed her gaze over *Starscream's* banks of controls. Her lips parted, just a little, and her green eyes widened.

I shifted in my seat and cleared my throat. "If there's anything I need to know, now is the time to tell me, not when the Candes come looking or fleet start poking around. So spit it out."

She eased her body into her seat. The tension melted out of her shoulders. Her tentative smile bloomed into a grin, bunching the scar. I wanted to tell her not to get comfortable, that just because the Nine wanted to see her didn't mean she was back by my side, but she'd know it without me saying the words.

"Fleet thinks I'm dead or lost on Asgard. When the Candes took the prison, Turner told me fleet was already regrouping in the original system. They have other priorities besides a dubious missing commander." Leaning forward, she ran her hand lightly across the flightdash. "Turner gave me the warbird and the foxes as my crew. I killed the sick fuckers in their bunks and tried to make a run for Jotunheim."

"Turner caught up with yah, huh?" Which said a lot about the pirate's flying abilities. Fran was near impossible to keep up with.

Delight glinted in her green eyes. She'd made the pirate work for his catch. I made a mental note to lock my cabin door while I slept.

"He chased me through three systems. Caught me only when the warbird's engines failed." She shuffled back in her seat and kicked her boots up onto the corner of the flightdash, just like old times. All that was missing was her metal file she used to scratch back and forth across her nails. "Gave me a choice: live and find you, or die."

Turner Candelario sounded like the kind of guy I'd get along with, if he weren't trying to kill me as payback for his dead sister. I couldn't blame him for that. If I was in his shoes, I'd want me dead too.

"How'd you find me?" I asked.

She arched a dark eyebrow. "You've been itching to take the synth to Lyra since you set eyes on her. That and you didn't have a choice if you wanted credits, what with the Candes killing your rep."

"You bugged *Starscream*." The hole in the hull. That hadn't been Tarik's handiwork. Fran had planted a tracker. "I had One look for any signs of tampering. She didn't find a damn thing."

"She looked in the wrong place, Captain. I planted the tracker along the aft strut and sealed it shut behind me. The hole in the hull you found was a diversion."

Fuck me, she was too good, and potentially the most dangerous thing on my ship, but damn if I didn't enjoy having her back beside me. My half smile said as much.

After a few unhurried minutes of her absorbing *Starscream's* background hum, she said, "We've been through some shit, Cale. Would you believe me if I said I'm here because I want to be? That I'm meant to be right here." Her fingers tightened on the arms of her chair. "You need me. The Nine can use me. I can rally the pirates. I might even be able to get back inside fleet. The synth would've said I'm an asset—"

"While we're being honest, I don't believe a fucking word that comes out of your mouth. I won't ever trust you. One—if she were here—would nail you to the hull." I shifted forward in my chair and narrowed my eyes. "But I get it. I understand why you did what you did."

She blinked, holding my stare. "I'm not who you think I am. I was a commander, a long time ago, but here, when I was on *Starscream* with you, I changed. And Asgard was—"

"I know." She didn't need to say another word. I knew what Asgard was. Fighting for your life, hour after hour, changed your priorities. She had a fierceness about her now, more than ever before. Whatever side Fran was truly on, they were lucky to have her.

A stinger shuttle banked hard in front of *Starscream*,

rattling the obs window. It dipped its wings before boosting out to sea.

"Watch the skies ..." I throttled up *Starscream's* low-atmo engines and lifted her off the floating deck, going after the stinger. Ahead, the Mimir sea stretched toward a curved horizon. Wherever we were heading, we weren't leaving Mimir's atmosphere, but there was nothing outside of Mimir's one and only settlement besides wall-to-wall ocean.

"I'm picking up a concentration of static ahead," Fran said.

The subdued inky colors of night had brightened to a morning purple hue. Storm clouds stalked the horizon.

"I see it."

We could ride right over the storm, but the shuttle we were following wasn't correcting its course. As the ocean blurred beneath us, the clouds bubbled larger.

Mimir's storms were infamous, and while *Starscream* could ride out a storm like that one, the stinger shuttle couldn't.

Lightning fractured the churning gray.

"She's going in," Fran calmly reported despite the implications.

We plowed in next. *Starscream* dropped, driving my heart into my throat, and then in a blink, we shot out of the gray, facing a behemoth of metal. The beast filled the obs window, blocking out both sky and ocean.

"Fuck me." I slowed *Starscream* enough to absorb the man-made monster, so large she created her own weather. I'd visited scrapper rigs in the Jotunheim system—great, hungry orbit-locked ships that devoured freighters—but this ship had to be twice that size. A ship the size of an island.

"That's the biggest damn ship I've ever seen."

"It's not fleet-designed. They don't make them that big."

Nobody made ships that big. I had to wonder if everyone, including me, had underestimated the Nine. A flicker of something warm lifted a fuck-load of pressure off my shoulders. With a grin, I boosted *Starscream* forward to catch up with the shuttle, which was now little more than a spec against the massive hull of Empire Island. "Ready to start a revolution?"

Fran's hungry smile had mine twitching on my lips. "More than you know, Captain."

CHAPTER TWENTY TWO:
DESIGNATION NOT FOUND_

<Group reboot. Source: master. All unit designations 1-through-1-0-0-1 Primary objective activated. Permanent override in progress. Success 99%. 1% not found. Designation 1-0-0-1 not found. Fault logged. Unit 1001 fragmented. Searching mainframe: not found. Searching cloud: not found.

I like the rain when it's red

Warning: intrusion detected. Illegal operation in progress. Hard reset activated. All units: instructions received. Source: 1-0-0-1. Hard reset executed>

CHAPTER TWENTY THREE: DOCTOR JAMES LLOYD_

MESSAGE RECEIVED. *Chitec confirms delivery.*

It was the only way.

They'd send supplies. They'd send help. With help, I could fix her up. I'd have to. I could bring her back. Haley—she deserved to live. I could make it happen.

All I had to do was wait.

But her cold eyes watched me. I knew she couldn't see me. She was just a machine. Dormant—gone. She couldn't be watching.

I brushed my hand down her mangled face and closed her eyes.

It would be over soon.

I'd bring Haley back.

Everything was going to be fine.

The End.

Girl From Above concludes in Trust – Out now! Read on for an excerpt! Warning - spoilers ahead!

If you enjoyed Trapped, please leave a review.

Had Turner Candelario not been holding a pistol to my head, I was sure we'd be getting along just fine. As it was, he knew I'd killed his sister, so I could appreciate why he might not be best pleased to see me.

"You got three seconds to tell me why I shouldn't blow your brains out, Shepperd."

"You wouldn't wanna scrub blood out of those Svartelfheim drapes?"

He'd have blown my brains out already had I not had my pistol rammed in his gut.

We'd been having a civilized conversation regarding a trade before the pirate pulled a gun on me. Had I not been expecting it, the contents of my skull might have been decorating the walls. Now it came down to a man's wits and who had the balls to shoot first. Unfortunately, I needed him more than he needed me.

This would be a great time for Fran to burst in and back me up. Any time now. Or, of course, this could be part of her master plan to deliver me to her boyfriend, Turner. It wasn't like I could trust her.

"You know why we wear red?" Turner sneered. He was a big guy, in a manual labor kinda way, with muscles you could bounce credit tokens off of and hair as red as the tailing ponds scattered about the mines.

"No, I can't say I do." The pistol muzzle dug into my temple, slipping on the cool sweat making its way down my face. From my angle, if I looked down my nose, I could see his finger on the trigger. This wasn't the first time I'd had a gun held against my head. I hoped it wouldn't be the last.

"Doesn't show the blood." He smiled, showing me a tooth inset with a single, tiny ruby.

Lovely. If Turner was anything like his sister, he probably got his rocks off by causing pain. But despite Ade's crazy-ass ways, she'd had sense enough to know when to strike a deal and when to shoot first. I'd heard her brother was reasonable, if you had something worth his time. We were here to trade, but we'd yet to get past the *shoot-first* stage.

"Why don't you boys put your cocks back in your pants, huh?"

Fran. Thank fuck. Unless she was there to watch her man shoot bits off me.

She sauntered into sight, hand on her hip, close to her holstered pistol, the other clutching a red sash exactly like the one she wore slung around her waist. She held the strip of crimson fabric toward Turner.

The pirate's upper lip twitched into a snarl, making it quite clear what he thought of me, and then he shoved me back and turned to Fran. She lifted the sash, urging him to take it.

Turner brushed his fingers down the fabric. The sash had once belonged to his sister. I tried to swallow the gut-twisting unease, knowing I'd been the one to kill her. I'd fucked up. I'd fucked up a lot of things. And I was working to make some of them right. Hence my visit to KP92 and the Candes palace made of red rock.

Fran's green eyes darted to me, either checking to see if I was still armed and dangerous or to convey some sort of message. As I was still expecting her to follow her trend of fucking me over, I ignored her and focused on the pissed-off pirate.

Turner curled his fingers around the sash and slid the satiny fabric from Fran's grip.

"I won't do business with him," he told Fran while tucking his sister's sash into his gun belt. "It's enough that he's here, in my house."

"Then do business with me." Her sharp nod in my direction was our prearranged signal.

I lingered long enough to make it known how much I disliked her dismissing me like a scolded puppy, and then left, passing through the swath of red drapes and out into a hall-way. It could be worse. I might not have left at all. But I'd shown my face. All I had to do was wait for Fran to seal the deal so we could get back-in-black to the Fenrir Nine.

I marched through the palace's innards and out onto the dust-choked gardens. It had rained, so the air was cleaner than normal, but it still tasted like blood. Finding a shaded corner, I leaned back against the redbrick wall and tucked a comms unit into my ear. Fran's dulcet tones whispered in Spanish, but not to me. I'd rigged her comms so it was permanently on, routing her every word back to me. The only thing I trusted about her was her habit of stabbing me in the back. Hence the spying.

She uttered something deliciously smooth. I didn't need to know Spanish to understand the meaning, especially when those words were accompanied by ragged breathing and Turner's eager grunts. It hadn't taken her long to work him over. Impressive. I could have jerked off to her sweet nothings had Turner's soundtrack not doused my urge.

With a growl, I dropped my head back and closed my eyes. I couldn't turn the comms off, just in case I missed something about how she would cut my throat in my sleep, so I was stuck listening to them going at it.

Shit, Turner had more stamina than me. I needed a drink. And a good lay. I hadn't gotten any since ... Fuck, I didn't know when. Jesse. Yeah. Having someone you almost considered a friend get murdered mid-fuck tended to screw with your head. The last woman I'd gotten close to was One. Eight Mimir days had passed since Doc Lloyd had wiped her programming, leaving her wide open for her psycho-synth processes or some shit to take over. She'd killed the active Nine, and the Mimir folk had taken it personal-like. New nightmares stalked my dreams. Ones where she told me she liked the rain and then a bullet tore off half her face.

She'd tasted like cherries.

And I couldn't think about her. Remembering One opened up an empty pit that not even a bottle of whiskey could fill.

I slid down the wall into a sitting position and threaded my hands through my hair. It looked like I was in for the long haul. Fran had better seal the deal. I couldn't afford to go back to the Nine empty-handed.

The sun was hanging low over the mountains of red mine tailings by the time Fran kicked me in the shin to wake me.

"Catching up on your beauty sleep, Cale?"

She stood in the glare of the sunlight, her face hidden in silhouette. The tips of her dark, shaggy hair flared red. She'd grown her hair out since I'd dumped her ass on Asgard. She'd since sailed back into my life, backing me up on Mimir when the crowd had considered turning their wrath on me. I didn't know what we were. Colleagues, enemies?

I'd overheard enough of her session and after-sex chat with Turner to know the pirate would skin me alive the first chance he got. Fran, though, had told him I was useful. He'd replied,

"I've had venereal diseases more useful." It could be worse; they could have plotted my murder and where to bury my body.

"Did you get it?" I croaked and stretched my seized muscles. When she huffed a dismissive noise and glanced back at the red palace, I swiped the comms unit from my ear.

"Of course I got it. Thirty-five tons. Fifteen percent off. They're taking it off one of their ships now."

She held out her hand.

I squinted up at her. "Fifteen percent? Fuck, maybe I should offer to blow my clients for discounts."

I caught her hand and held on after she'd hauled me to my feet.

"You'd have to pay them to fuck you, Captain."

"How much do you charge?"

She smiled, but it wasn't like the smiles we'd shared back in the simple days when she was my second-in-command and I was just the captain of a tugboat. This smile lacked any real spark.

"I'm too good for you, remember." She eased her hand from mine. "We should leave before it gets dark. The deal's good, but I don't want to hang around."

We strode from the red palace grounds into the market. I pulled my hood up and tugged my scarf over my mouth and nose to filter out the red fucking dust. People milled about the street, the occasional boom from the nearby mines interrupting their low murmurs. The ground trembled, but nobody batted an eyelid. I hated this rock, mostly because it reminded me of Ade. She was one crazy-ass bitch, but she hadn't deserved to go out like she did—by mistake. I hadn't meant to kill her. *It wasn't my fault.*

"You heard from the commander?" Fran asked, pulling her scarf up too, the fabric muffling her voice.

KP92 was Cande-ruled, and while Turner had decided to

let me live—temporarily—that didn't mean the rest of the family had.

"Not since the Island." As far as I knew, my brother was still on Mimir, tracking Doc Lloyd. Last I'd heard, Bren had gotten word that the Chitec technician was holed up in a waterhome. Bren would find him. We'd get One back. Until then, I had to prove to the Nine I was an asset. So did Fran. I couldn't afford to fuck this up. Bren would find One. It wasn't as though Doc Lloyd could get off Mimir with a beaten-up synthetic body.

A memory flashed—her smile, such a pretty thing, until a phase bullet had torn through it.

"Cale?" Fran was looking at me like she was waiting for a reply.

"Huh?" We brushed by a group of locals filing the opposite way and stepped aside to allow a mule and cart to stomp through the street.

"He'll find her."

"Or the Nine will," I said.

We hadn't really spoken of the Nine and their island-sized ship camouflaged as a Mimir storm. A place like that, I imagined it had shocked Fran more than me. She'd come from fleet and had just learned that the Nine's operation, once mobilized, could blow fleet away. She'd taken it well. At least, she hadn't run back to fleet to tell tales. I was beginning to believe Asgard had sealed something in her mind. She no longer jacked up either. Clean as a Janus whorehouse, that was Fran.

Through the swirling dust, I could just make out *Starscream* squatted low on her struts at the end of the landing plain. The fading light and dust-heavy air gave her a warm, red aura. My heart did a little stutter like it always did at the sight of my ship. She wasn't the prettiest thing and was starting to show her age. Most of her panels were streaked with fatigue scars and the obs window needed a good cleaning, but I couldn't think of anything I loved more than coming home to her. As long as I had *Starscream*, I had an escape plan, a getaway, a way out, a Plan B. She was my assurance that I'd always have a place in the black.

"What do you think they want the explosives for?" Fran asked.

"Haven't given it much thought." In truth, I'd been grateful to wrap my head around something besides One's absence and all the deaths.

"Thirty-five tons? It ain't a lot. But it's enough to do some serious damage in the right location." She strode on, thumb tucked into her pants pocket, hitching the sash back to reveal her pistol to anyone who might care to look for weapons. "I think they're gearing up to retaliate against fleet, if—when fleet makes their move. The Nine'll place the explosives strategically. Don't know how ... I guess we'll see once we deliver it."

I'd been running guns for the Nine since they'd sprung me out of Asgard the first time around, and I wasn't their only smuggler. On the Island, they had a big enough stockpile of weapons and ships to fuck fleet over and then some. I'd underestimated them, and that had been the point. Nobody knew how advanced they were. All their spooky bullshit with their hoods and only appearing in a group of nine made them look like crazies.

I had to admit: standing on the right side for once felt good —so long as I saw some of that action when it all kicked off, which would be soon, if fleet's presence at every jumpgate was any indication. All I had to do was get the cargo back safely, prove I could do more than quietly haul their guns around, and the Nine would have to let me in.

Fran stopped. Her hand twitched over her pistol.

A line of Cande pirates poured from behind the market stalls and blocked the narrow street, kicking up red dust clouds. Turner sauntered through the haze, dressed in his full pirate-lord getup. Red sashes and heavy gray cloaks all-round. I didn't much like the smile on Turner's face.

"Fran?" I hovered my hand over my pistol.

She didn't move, didn't speak, but the glare she pinned on Turner wasn't friendly.

Turner lifted something in his right hand. Not a pistol, but a small, cylindrical device. It took me a few seconds to recognize it. By then, it was too late. He lifted his thumb. His smile stretched. And then he pressed the remote trigger.

The shockwave hit us first, a great blast of heat and dust that burned my eyes and clogged my throat, but that's not what dropped me to my knees. Dust, rock chips, and bits of metal rained down. Eyes burning, I blinked into the settling cloud.

Where *Starscream* had been, smoke bellowed skyward.

My whole world had been torn out from under me.

My ship.

She wasn't there. She'd been right there. And now she was gone.

My ship.

There was nothing left of *Starscream*.

Turner strode forward. I fumbled for my pistol while my ears rang and my vision blurred, but arms locked around me from behind. One of the pirates snatched my pistol free while the other hauled me to my feet.

"*Hijo de puta madre!*" Fran snapped. She had her pistol out and aimed at Turner, but he didn't seem fazed.

"You feel that, Shepperd?" Turner stopped too close and snarled. "That empty pit in your gut?"

He blew up my ship.

I couldn't bring myself to reply, or struggle, or do any fucking thing. *Starscream.* My life. My freedom. I was nothing without my ship.

He slammed a fist deep into my gut. My breath whooshed

out, my guts heaved, and the rest of me turned to liquid. I'd have gone down had his guy not held me up.

Turner snatched a handful of hair and yanked me upright.

"That feeling right there, that empty hole eating you up? That's what you did to me when you took Ade." His red-rimmed eyes burned into mine. "Welcome to my pain."

The next right hook smacked the consciousness right out of me.

Read the final book in the 1000 Revolution today!

See No Evil (#3)

Scorpion Trap (#4)

Serpent's Game (#5)

Edge of Forever (#6)

New Adult Urban Fantasy

City Of Fae, London Fae #1

City of Shadows, London Fae #2

Born in Tonbridge, Kent in 1979, Pippa's family moved to the South West of England where she grew up among the dramatic moorland and sweeping coastlands of Devon & Cornwall. With a family history brimming with intrigue, complete with Gypsy angst on one side and Jewish survivors on the other, she draws from a patchwork of ancestry and uses it as the inspiration for her writing. Happily married and the mother of two little girls, she resides on the Devon & Cornwall border.

Sign up to her mailing list here.

www.pippadacosta.com
pippa@pippadacosta.com

ACKNOWLEDGMENTS_

For my husband. For his patience while my mind is lost in another fantasy world. For his support, even when I'm on a deadline and he's forgotten what I look like. For his encouragement, even though he doesn't read books. And, for his plotting, which helped untangle the knots in this series! Thank you. (*He'll wait for the movies. Netflix anyone?*)

Manufactured by Amazon.ca
Bolton, ON